MURDERS ON DEATH ROW

By

Michael Ramos

Disclaimer

The author has made every effort to ensure the accuracy of the information presented in this book; however, errors and omissions may occur. Readers are advised to use their own discretion and judgment while interpreting the content.

This book is a work of fiction. Names, characters, businesses, organizations, places, events, and incidents either are the product of the author's imagination or are used fictitiously. Any resemblance to actual persons, living or dead, events, or locales is entirely coincidental.

Dedication

To all victims of crime and their family members.

Acknowledgment

I would like to thank my family and friends and all those involved in the justice system for your support. A special thanks to Heidi Mackumul for her great typing and formatting skills and to my daughter-in-law, Allyson Ramos for her editing.

Table Of Contents

PART II MIAMI

PART III THE STORM

PART IV 2006 THE PUZZLE

PART V FLORENCE, ITALY 2006

PART VI THE END

PART I

Chapter 1

2004

As Deputy District Attorneys, we take an oath to uphold the Constitution of the United States and, more importantly, conduct ourselves in the highest ethical manner as decisions we make will impact individuals for the rest of their lives. Prosecuting an innocent person is something we never want to do.

After Christine shocked me and the local community and beyond, for that matter, I went to work to release the convicted individual I tried for murder. I never thought in my life that a "nobody" murder case would actually result in a victim who was alive all along. That only happens in the movies. Even though Christine Stone had been missing for thirty years, she was alive and well, living a great life in Italy.

I immediately petitioned the Court to have the convicted inmate, Clyde Baker, released from prison. The detectives on the case were just as shocked, but they understood. We speculated that the bones of the person found in the silos of Okieville may have been Clyde Baker's brother, Jessie. The killer? Mr. Stone, the father of Christine, for bullying and assaulting his daughter, Christine. However, he was now dead, and the "cold case" was closed.

I did feel bad for the justice system. I was happy for Mrs. Stone, who had not seen her daughter for decades. I guess we did some good.

While sitting at my desk, there was a knock on my door. "Come in." In walked Detective Dean Liter. "What's up?" He liked to start his serious conversations with "Houston, we have a problem," a quote from NASA's Apollo 13 crew.

Chapter 2

2004

Detective Liter was wearing his Seattle Seahawks baseball cap as he sat across my desk, knowing I was a Rams fan going back to my childhood and "Roman Gabriel."

"Tony, a retired teacher and coach, was found murdered. His wife discovered his body in the front yard of their home on their sidewalk with a newspaper in his hand around 6:00 a.m. I wanted you to hear it from me before the press and social media start their reporting. I'm glad you were here early today."

I came into the office at 6:30 a.m. to finish some paperwork regarding our last case. Detective Liter said the homicide team was at the crime scene as we spoke and wanted me to be there as well. "Of course," I said, "let's go!"

We jumped into Detective Liter's Ford Crown Vic and raced to the scene in Redlands, California, the same community I lived in. My thoughts and prayers were with my former coach and his family, and I could not stop thinking about our last talk. After my last trial, he asked me at church (both of us being Catholic), if I was ready to be the District Attorney. Coach Greg Rogers was my high school defensive coordinator and was a good man.

When we first arrived, I immediately went to find Mrs. Rogers. As I approached the house, the body was covered up with yellow evidence placards spread all over the front yard. As I lifted the evidence tape surrounding the front yard of their beautiful home and entered the front door, I found Mrs. Rogers sitting in her living room with her only son, Greg Jr.

As she stood sobbing, I gave her a hug and told her how sorry I was. She was still in her robe and pajamas and looked like she had

2

been crying for hours. Detective Sandy Smith from the homicide team had already interviewed her, and my role was only to provide comfort and to let her know we have the best homicide team in the country on the case and, if possible, I would be handling the case, as a major crime unit prosecutor. She said, "If possible? My husband said you were the best. He truly had so much respect for you, Anthony."

I left the living room area and met Detective Liter out front. The crime lab was now present and combing the entire home and yard for forensic evidence. I told him I would like to get back to the office as I wanted to brief District Attorney Matthews before the press called. On the ride back, Detective Liter told me it was early in the investigation, but they did know he was shot with a 9mm handgun, and the shooter was pretty advanced, hitting him in the chest and another round to the head. They will determine what round hit first, if possible. Gun residue on the head would indicate a very close shot. That was yet to be determined.

As I was dropped off, Dean Liter said, "I guess no golf anytime soon."

I said, "It sure doesn't look like it."

"I'll get back to you, Tony, as soon as we finish up with the crime scene."

"Sounds good, as DA Matthews may assign me the case."

Chapter 3

1975

It was the fall of 1975; we were playing Anaheim High School in a pre-season football game at Angel Stadium. I was playing both running back and split side defensive end at 5'7 and 150 pounds soaking wet, but I ran the 40-yard dash in 4.6 seconds and could bench press 250 pounds. Not bad for a skinny little brown boy, my teammates would say. Ha! The team we were playing ran a wishbone offense, and Coach Rogers had prepared us for this rivalry and their offense. Coach Rogers had told me my only job was to hit their quarterback as early as possible when he came my way with the ball. The stands were full and loud for being in this big stadium. I was excited, as were all my teammates. We won the toss and elected to get the ball first. Our quarterback was awesome, but we needed to establish the run game before he could start slinging away. The first play was called, and it was time to go to work. We were in power I, and "student body right" was called, a sweep by me to the right side. As I got the ball, I had a great block, made a good first move on the linebacker, and gained fourteen yards on the first play of the game. On the next play, quarterback John Couch hit wide receiver Peters on a post pattern for a touchdown. It was a great way to start the game and the season. The game ended up being closer than we liked, but we won 17-14 on a last-minute forty-seven-yard field goal. I'll always remember Coach Rogers hugging and picking me up, saying I played a great game. On the bus ride home, Elton John's *Yellow Brick Road* was playing, and we were all singing "Saturday Nights All Right." It was a Saturday game, after all.

The next morning, the headline in the local newspaper was "Anthony Garcia had a good game playing both ways," with a picture of Coach Roger's arm around my back.

My pops said, "Great game, boy, but it is time to get to church, and we need to go visit Grandma Garcia after mass." I loved that, as I could already smell the fresh flour tortillas being made with her homemade frijoles and eggs.

Life was good!

Chapter 4

2004

As I sat back in my office, I looked at a framed picture I love. A picture of me, number 87, running with the football against Anaheim High School. It brought back memories of my favorite teacher and coach, Greg Rogers. Who and why would someone take his life? I was determined to find out.

I looked over at my desk phone and saw the message light blinking. As I hit the play button, it was from my good friend, Dave, from the Attorney General's Office.

"Tony, I hope you're doing well. I'm calling to talk to you about two murders that took place on death row at San Quentin Prison, and both killers are from your County. One is a serial killer, and the other is a cop killer. The Marin County District Attorney says she does not have the resources to file and prosecute the cases, and we certainly do not have the resources. We would like to hire you as a special prosecutor; call me when you can."

My day just got crazier. I then began to research the cases through social media. I know this: they would not be looked at as your typical murder victims; in fact, most would say justice was served.

I found an article in the San Francisco Chronicle. There was not much detail regarding their murder convictions, but I can look them up here in the office. What did stand out was both killers died of potassium chloride, a chemical that stops the heart and is used in the three-drug protocol for death by lethal injection. Well, if the State doesn't do it, someone else is taking care of business.

Before I did any more research, I decided to call my friend at the Attorney General's Office back. As I was about to make the call, in walked my boss, DA Matthews.

"Anthony, I just got off the phone with the Attorney General, Ann Baker. She was reaching out to me regarding the murders on death row. I'm sure you've heard of them. They are looking for a 'special prosecutor' to cross-designate as a Deputy A.G. as they do not have the expertise to take on this case. My first thought was you, as your reputation as a trial lawyer is known statewide, and you are a co-chair of the California District Attorneys Association Homicide Committee."

I said I would do it, but I would like to keep the murder of my old high school coach, Mr. Rogers. He agreed. I also had one other request. I wanted to cross-designate Detective Dean Liter as a Department of Justice Special Investigator to help with the case. District Attorney Matthews said he would call the Sheriff. Of course, I hadn't asked Dean yet, but I know him, and I'm sure he would agree.

I called my buddy at the Attorney General's Office back and said, "You'll be seeing me soon." He was excited.

I then called Detective Liter. I asked him if he remembered the sand shot he hit out of the fairway bunker for an Eagle. He replied he did. I then told him I had a tougher shot for him. How would he like to work with me on the "Death Row" murders? He asked if he had a choice. I said, "No." He laughed and said he couldn't wait; plus, he loved hanging out in San Francisco.

Chapter 5

1976

It was a typical spring day, and you could smell the orange blossoms off the hundreds of trees surrounding our community. It was Saturday, and my ex-Marine father had my brothers and me doing our weekly chores, both inside and outside of our home. We flipped a coin on who would edge the front lawn as that was done with an "idiot stick." You know, the one with a long stick and a roller with blades on the end. It was not fun, but it sure did the trick, like the lines on a baseball infield. But the best part of the morning was when we were all done, and my dad took us to his local bar down the street in Mentone, where they made these amazing wet burritos—meat, beans, and cheese, covered with a delicious red enchilada sauce. Of course, we had an ice-cold Coke while my father enjoyed a beer to start his afternoon—a great tradition.

Later that day, I had band practice with our garage band, "Mighty Mike," named after our lead guitar player, Mike Hernandez. He could shred his Les Paul like no other. Most of us were athletes: our drummer, Pete, was a good basketball player, and I was playing rhythm guitar and the lead singer. We were a cover band working on some new songs for a gig we were doing in a week at a Spring Break party. On our list were Red Bone's "Come and Get Your Love" and several other songs that were current hits, including Peter Frampton, Steely Dan, and a few Santana songs for the "vatos" out there. It was fun, but I knew this might be my last gig as I had some other goals besides music.

My girlfriend, Rachel, was much more disciplined than I was. We had been dating for over a year now, and she got a job at a local drive-thru taco burger joint that we all loved. And she was an excellent student. I loved it when she came by the house after getting off work. She smelled like a taco, and we would laugh as I begged for a hug. Of course, on that Saturday morning, she was taking the SAT in preparation for her goal to attend college. While I was jamming and enjoying, a little "Green stuff" rolled up like my grandpa's "Prince Albert" cigarettes. It was at this time that I decided I wanted to further my education as well. I was no Paul McCartney, and it was time to be real. She inspired me, plus I got free red burritos at her place of work, and I did not want to screw that up! HA!

A week later, we were playing at the party in Okieville, in my good buddy's backyard, with keg beer flowing and over two hundred Spring Break teenagers having fun. Along with Rachel and her posse, we had many friends there, including Cathy Diaz, who was dating Mike at the time. She was a lot of fun but could get a little wild at times, with tonight being no exception. She was dancing away, and between sets, she was hanging out with us on our breaks, talking about how rude some out-of-town boys were. We told her to shake it off as we were amongst friends. We did know that a party this big brought fools from all over the place. However, most were from our hometown.

Rachel was having a great time dancing with her girlfriends, as you know who was in the band. As the night ended, we all decided to jump in Rachel's '64 Buick and head to Denny's for an after-party breakfast. Nothing like a chicken fried steak to soak up some keg beer.

As we got there, Mike said, "Where's Cathy?" Mike had driven there with another group of friends. We said, "We thought she was with you."

She must've gone home, or did she?

Chapter 6

2004

I started to go back and look at both inmates' murder convictions by pulling their files from our storage facility. Luckily, both cases were in their original trial boxes, and both were very well organized. It did not surprise me as both of these individuals were tried by one of the best prosecutors of his time, Deputy District Attorney John Lockwood.

I opened the first box, and it was all labeled per witness. The first inmate was Doug Jones, who was convicted of several murders that occurred in three different counties, the last one being in ours. All the victims were in their late teens and were found bludgeoned and strangled to death. The case was cross-designated to prosecute them all in our county, as the first two cases occurred in the neighboring Counties of Los Angeles and Riverside.

Of course, I remembered the case like it was yesterday. I was a senior in high school when Cathy Diaz went missing for several days and was found by a hiker in the Santa Ana River. We were all shocked, and my best friend, Mike Hernandez, along with my girlfriend, now wife Rachel, were all devastated. She was Mike's girlfriend at the time, and he still feels guilty to this day that he was not there to protect her.

Her body was found below a railroad bridge crossing, lying on the rocks below, with the river water flowing over her legs as her head and upper torso were twisted on the rocks. The San Bernardino County Sheriff's Office had done a great job gathering evidence. The killer made several mistakes. One, a bottle of Coors beer, was found at the scene with his fingerprints all over it. Two, he had dropped a piece of rope that was used to strangle Cathy. A Search Warrant of the killer's home found the same rope type cut off at one end. The same rope that was used to kill his other two victims.

10

When he was arrested, he confessed to all three killings, saying he was about to kill again if he had not been caught. A true serial killer!

Inmate number 2—Richard Cruz. It was 1990, and he was a career criminal, having served two prison terms, one for a robbery and the second for a Felon in Possession of a Handgun. The victim was CHP Officer Mark Chavez. At the time, suspect Cruz had a Bench Warrant for his arrest issued for another Robbery that took place in Rialto, California. A 911 call was made regarding a motorist on the 10 Freeway attempting to side-swipe other vehicles. Officer Chavez responded to the call and saw the suspect's vehicle driving erratically, heading East on the 10 Freeway. Officer Chavez went to Code 3 (lights and sirens) and began his pursuit. Right before the Ford Street off-ramp in Redlands, the suspect, in response to Officer Chavez's red lights and siren, pulled his vehicle over on the right shoulder. Luckily, Officer Chavez's patrol vehicle had a camera located on the front window panel.

As Officer Chavez approached the suspect's vehicle, he had his duty weapon on his right-hand side. He yelled out for the driver to exit the vehicle with his hands up. Before exiting his vehicle, Officer Chavez had called in for backup, a smart move. As the suspect exited his vehicle, he raised a gun, firing several rounds at Officer Chavez. Officer Chavez was hit in the leg and in the neck area but was able to return fire, wounding the suspect in the leg. Officer Chavez did not survive his wounds. As backup Officers arrived, the suspect attempted to flee up a hill on the south side of the freeway, where he collapsed from the gunshot wound to his right leg. He was arrested and convicted of First-Degree Murder with the Use of a Firearm and the Special Circumstance that he killed a Peace Officer in the Line of Duty. Again, my thoughts were no loss to society, but the cases must be investigated and prosecuted if possible.

My first thought was that the family members of both victims they murdered be notified. That would be my first priority. I'll call Dave at the Attorney General's Office to see if that has occurred.

As I was about to call him, in walked Detective Liter, "Tony, we have an update on Coach Rogers' murder."

Chapter 7

1976

Our senior year was full of fun and excitement, as well as the pain of losing one of our dear friends, Cathy Diaz. Our class President, Lloyd Haskins, was going to give the keynote address at our graduation ceremony. He was a great choice and friend. In fact, he was friends with everyone from the athletes to the surfers and the "cool" kids. When I say cool, they really were with their long hair, Ocean Pacific, "OP" shirts, and Led Zeppelin followers. I spent many weekends partying with these friends, waking up to a "Tequila Sunrise" at times. Yes, we were living "life in the fast lane." Lloyd had several of these parties at his parent's home, and they were really cool about it as they would rather see their kids and friends at their home than out in the orange groves having a party. The times were good, and we were all excited about the next chapters in our lives.

At the last party we had, the week before graduation, a few of our coaches showed up. This was in the early afternoon, of course. My favorite Coach, Rogers, was one of them and gave me some good news that the local junior college, San Bernardino Valley College's football coach was interested in me. They had been undefeated for the last two years and were a portal to many four-year programs. I was not sure yet if I wanted to continue playing football, but it was nice to be wanted. I asked Coach Rogers about my other teammates. We knew our quarterback was going to Arizona State but were unsure about the others. It was at that time that he told me about one of our all-league linebackers, who was recruited by USC, and others had been arrested for the sale of cocaine, and it was Coach Rogers who had caught him selling to other students during a pep rally for the baseball team. We all wondered why he was not in school the last month. It was then I realized how fast you can throw your life away. Drugs were all over the place; with the exception of Marijuana, I stayed clear. I saw how it was destroying kids' lives, plus my dad would kill me.

I could tell Coach Rogers felt bad about it, but I told him he did the right thing, and I thanked him for all he had done for me.

Graduation was a blast. Lloyd gave a great speech about our class and where we were going in the future. We then did the traditional Disneyland trip on a bus with all our friends for a night of fun. Oh, and it was fun until a classmate threw up in the back of the bus on the way home. The song "In My Life" by the Beatles will always remind me of these places, friends, and the memories we cherished.

Chapter 8

2004

"Dean, have a seat. It's good you stopped by as I was trying to wrap my head around Coach Rodgers' murder."

"Well, Tony, we found the gun that was used in the orange groves behind the new high school that is located across the street from the victim's home." It was a Redlands Unified High School, but both Coach Roger's home and the school were located in the unincorporated region of San Bernardino County. "We took the weapon to the crime lab, and the ballistics matched the round we recovered at the scene of his murder, and we are now awaiting any fingerprint evidence. We also found that the shots fired were from a distance, as there was no gunpowder on the victim's wounds. There were also four other shots we missed that we found embedded in the stucco of the house and a tree in the front yard. Shoe prints were recovered in the groves that we are trying to compare to a shoe style. Whoever shot Coach Rogers was on foot."

At this time, I told him how yesterday it came back to me. "A teammate in high school named Travis Williams, a superstar football player whose life was destroyed by drugs. I heard he had done several stints in prison, and it started with Coach Rogers. I also recall him being on Felony Probation when I was a Probation Officer. Dean, you remember him, an arrest in Crestline."

"That's right, when I first met you, Tony."

"That's a lead we did not have. I'll pull his prior records, and let's hope the gun used had fingerprints. You want to get a beer later?"

"No, that's okay. I need to stop by and say hello to someone on the way home."

Being raised Catholic, I always found peace and strength going to church, even if there was no mass scheduled. Most of the time, Sacred Heart Church left its doors open, and I felt like the world slowed down when I was there. As I knelt to thank God for all his blessings, I also said prayers for the Rogers family and all the victims' families of the cases I have handled. And now those of the victims who were murdered, whose killers may have been murdered on Death Row.

As a Catholic, I struggled with the issue of the Death Penalty, but when you looked into the eyes and hearts of family members who lost loved ones to the worst of the worst killers, I still believed in the ultimate punishment. I recall one of our greatest Presidents, JFK, always talked about the separation of Church and State; at least, that's what Grandma Garcia said. I will always remember she had a picture of President Kennedy right next to a picture of the Virgin Mary. Not too separated if you ask me.

I got home just in time to change and get to soccer practice with my daughter. I coached an 18-year-old club soccer team, Redlands Hot Shots, another way to relieve tension. We were good and undefeated. My son was on his own team and was kicking 50-yard field goals for his football team. Tonight was my turn to prepare dinner after another long day: my go-to dinner, hot dog and bean burritos. I have to admit they were yummy. Tomorrow would be another interesting day.

Chapter 9

1977—1988

After high school, it seemed as if time flew by. Rachel and I attended San Bernardino Valley College together, and then we transferred to the University of California, Riverside. I played on a club rugby team, and we traveled all over Southern California for our matches. Our scrum half on the team, Paul Mullins, who became a very good friend, was attending law school at night and told me how much he was getting out of it. That was the first time I thought about becoming a lawyer. I still had nightmares of my good friend, Christine Stone, who had gone missing in the sixth grade, and Cathy Diaz, who we lost to a vicious killer. It was then that I decided I wanted to be a prosecutor. I felt that was the best way to help victims of crime.

After graduation, Rachel and I both received our bachelor's degrees in Sociology. She went to work for an insurance company, and I became a probation officer. A year later, our daughter, Christine, was born, and law school would have to be put on hold.

As a probation officer, I was assigned to the Major Crimes Unit for those on probation who were the most serious felons. One of my partners, Barry Truman, had the mountain area as his region of responsibility. One of the probationers who was giving him problems was Travis Williams, on probation for the sale of cocaine. Yes, the all-star linebacker I played with; his life had spun out of control. He was on the run, but we found him during a probation sweep. Probation officer Truman had not met him yet and had only heard a description of him, along with tattoos.

We entered a home in Crestline and found that several on parole and probation had been living there and were having a good time. Travis was there but used an alias as probation officer Truman and a backup Sheriff deputy Dean Liter, out of the Twin Peaks Station, were trying to identify who was who in this house of crooks. Unluckily for Travis, I stepped into the living room area. Travis looked at me and said, "F me." "Hey, Tony." "Hello, Travis." He was then arrested for a probation violation and a new felony. He had a handgun on him this time, which Dean Liter immediately found when he patted him down.

Not only did we make the community safer that day, but I made a friend and had a long-term professional relationship with Deputy Sheriff Dean Liter.

After several years as a probation officer, I came home one day and told Rachel I would like to go to law school at night. It would be a tough road as our second child was born, and I would continue to work full-time as a probation officer. She was always supportive, and the next four years were grueling but exciting at the same time. We both worked full-time. Thankfully, my Aunt Tense babysat our kids. We had a big family, and that helped. As I look back, it was like a "magical mystery tour," not knowing what the future held. But I did know that I wanted the best for my family, and I wanted to make a difference in this world. I passed the California Bar exam in the summer of 1988, and I went right to work for the District Attorney's Office. I had an offer from the Public Defender's Office as well, but frankly, I was tired of dealing with probationers, and my passion was for victims of crimes.

And so it began my life as a fighter for crime victims. This may sound corny, but my favorite show back in the day was the original "Batman" series. Yes, I felt like the caped crusader! P.O.W.!

Chapter 10

2004

It was time to take a trip to San Quentin. First, a little history was in order. I went to the library and looked up the history of this prison. Early history shows the prison's origin dates back to the California Gold Rush. It was a period between 1848 and 1852 that brought fortune seekers to the San Francisco area, but it also brought an increase in crime. The prison was built in 1854, originally featuring forty-eight windowless cells, which were designed to hold 250 inmates. The number expanded soon thereafter. At the time, the prison was run by a private firm. The abuse was everywhere: Inhumane living conditions, including punishments that included floggings and "shower baths," in which inmates were stripped and sprayed with a power hose. Security was lax as well. In 1854, more than eighty prisoners broke out of San Quentin. Reform came in the late 1800s as the State took control. Flogging and whippings were banned. From 1913—1925, improved medical treatment and the creation of educational and vocational training came about. Also, corporal punishment was replaced with solitary confinement.

In 1893, California's first state execution took place, the hanging of a convicted murderer in San Quentin. In 1938, the gas chamber was installed, and it remained there and was used until 1996, when lethal injection was adopted. It housed a number of serial killers, most notably Charles Manson. San Quentin was known throughout the world. Many songs, movies, and books were written about it.

Fast forward to 2004. We were about to meet the first woman warden in the history of the prison. Detective Liter and I made plans to fly out to San Francisco, stay in the city that doesn't sleep, and get to work.

We arrived on a Thursday evening and checked into a hotel near

Pier 33, Fisherman's Wharf. We were both craving the clam chowder they served in the Marina District. After we checked in, we were not disappointed. We went to my favorite restaurant, the "Slanted Door." The fresh clam chowder in a bread bowl was amazing. There was jazz music playing nearby, and it made the travel day worth it. We ended the evening at the "Buena Vista" for their world-renowned Irish Coffee.

The next morning, we jumped into our rental car to take the thirty-minute drive to San Quentin. There were over 740 men and women on death row, and now they had two fewer.

When we arrived, we were escorted in by a guard, and after clearing security, we were led to the warden's office. Mrs. Wendy Godfried, the first female warden at San Quentin. She was very professional and had a team ready to show us the cells of the two inmates who were found dead in their bunks. I asked if we could get "the lay of the land" with a quick tour first. To which she replied, "Of course you can."

We were surrounded by three guards as this was still the most dangerous prison in the country. To say that death row was dark and gloomy is an understatement. What hits you first is the smell. The odor of bleach and human feces that some mentally ill inmates smear on the walls of their cells.

Each inmate was in a single cell. Along the east side, block cells were stacked five high with narrow steel balconies watched over by armed officers on the catwalk, a narrow walk along the cells. Each cell had a concrete bed, but I was surprised that inmates could get mail daily and had books and magazines as well as snacks, radios, and 13-inch televisions. The cells were 13 feet long, 7 feet wide, and 8 feet high—not a lot of room. They get to get out for an hour a day if they choose to work out in a caged cell with a pull-up bar.

However, on the northside yard, a small number of best-behaved inmates are housed. From the basketball courts, they have a great view of the San Francisco Bay.

As we walked along the front of the cells, there were "cat calls." I guess that's why they call it a catwalk. One was from an inmate I had prosecuted for the murder of a young girl who was kidnapped while attending a slumber party. He was a career criminal and, as far as I was concerned, was one of the evilest individuals in the world. He did not disappoint in calling me a "skinny brown asshole" as we walked by. I tried to ignore him, but it was hard. On the other hand, I saw Detective Liter smile at him and give him the "you're number one" hand gesture. That's my buddy.

After the tour, we then went to the two cells of the inmates who were found dead on their bedding. The cells had been cleaned out, and Detective Liter and I looked at each other like we had just lost our minds. However, it was all good as their belongings were tagged into the prison's evidence room, including but not limited to all correspondence. That was going to be the first step, going through their stuff.

We then requested the names of the inmates close to them in proximity and the nature of their relationships, if any. We also wanted the names of the guards who worked the days before, and at the time the murders were discovered, as well as the prison shift schedule.

Our goal was to find out how they got the drug in their system that killed them and by whom. Could it be self-induced? In that case, there would be a fast conclusion to this investigation. Time will tell. One other thing I was surprised to learn was that they could have visitors, with a barrier, of course, unless it was with their attorneys. We requested the visitor logs as well.

21

The warden offered us a meeting room right next to her office to go over all the evidence. We told her that would work. I then asked if there was any chance we could get a coffee pot. Yes, I'm a caffeine addict. Detective Liter was just happy with his cokes. Warden Godfried said there was one in there, along with various snacks. It was time to go to work.

The first thing we pulled was the visitor's log for these two killers; I mean "victims." It's even hard for me to put them in that box. Neither inmate Jones nor inmate Cruz had any visitors since being placed on death row, except their appellate lawyers. We would interview them at some point.

Inmate Jones had no letters except one from a rag newspaper that wanted to interview him for a series they were doing on serial killers. It did not appear that he responded to it.

Inmate Cruz, on the other hand, had several letters from his mother and some other family members. Not much was said except for the typical "How are you?" and telling him about the family and his mother putting money in his books. Inmate Cruz also had several art pieces he had done with pencil. Many with religious themes, apparently, he had found God. I guess it's better late than never.

We worked up until around 5:00 p.m. When the warden said it was time to close the shop, we decided we would be back early tomorrow. Before she walked in, we were reviewing the names of the prison guards who worked during the hours before and after the deaths.

Detective Liter looked at me and said, "You're not going to believe this shit, Tony." "What?"

"One of the guards' names is David Chavez!" Cruz's victim was Officer Mark Chavez. "It is a common name, but could they be related? Let's find out!"

After getting back to our hotel room, we decided to walk down to the wharf for dinner. Lobster tails and cold beers were in order. As we sat down to eat, Dean looked at me and said in his "Columbo" imitation, "Tony, I've been trying to figure out who has access to the drug Potassium Chloride" as he rubbed his cocked head, "and how was it administered?"

"Great question, Columbo. We need to get the autopsy reports next."

"Sounds good."

The lobster and fresh sourdough bread were delicious, and the beer was ice cold. I was looking forward to another busy day tomorrow.

Just at that moment, my phone rang. It was my daughter Christine. "Hey Chris, what's up?"

"Just checking in, Dad. Soccer practice is not fun without you, but we are working out hard. Mom and Patrick are at his football practice, and we are having pizza tonight."

"Well, I'm going to be here a couple of days, but I should be home for our soccer game on Saturday."

We said our goodbyes, and Dean and I headed back to our hotel as we had another long day ahead of us. When I got back to my hotel room, there was a package waiting for me. It was the reports, including the autopsy reports of both "victims."

The investigative reports were short, with little information. Both bodies were found on their beds, and the pictures looked like they died in their sleep. I guess that's why we were here to conduct the full investigation.

The autopsy report indicated what we already knew. Both died of heart attacks. There were no injection sites, not surprised, and the potassium chloride was taken orally. There was another drug in their systems as well called "Fentanyl," a new drug that was about to kill thousands across the country. I did my research on this drug. It can be used in small doses for individuals with very low potassium levels and is dissolved in water. A high dose can kill. The question remains: who and how?

Chapter 11

After a good night's rest, I was ready to roll. Liter and I agreed to meet for breakfast in the hotel café at 7:00 a.m. Yes, I call him by his last name most of the time, as that's what his partners call him. However, his other nickname is "EZ," like Easy, as he is cool, so they say.

The coffee was hot and delicious, and we both had some scrambled eggs and bacon as we discussed our plan for the day. Before we left the prison the night before, Warden Godfried was going to have the list of guards for us to interview first thing in the morning.

As we arrived at San Quentin, I could not help but think of all the victims and their families that put these men and a few women on death row. Again, I have met several of those family members, and I'm sure they're not concerned about these deaths.

As we checked in, we met with Warden Godfried and went into our "work" room with fresh coffee brewed. We had scheduled eight guards to be interviewed starting at 8:00 a.m., with Guard David Chavez being the last as he worked the swing shift from 4:00 p.m. to 12:00 a.m.

With the exception of a few details, the first seven guards we interviewed indicated they saw nothing unusual. They all indicated that both inmates stayed in their rooms, and it was rare. They even went out for their "exercise" hour. They were not problem inmates and basically kept to themselves. One guard did indicate he intercepted "kites" notes from prisoner to prisoner on several occasions, from inmate Cruz to inmate Jones. The topic was illegal drugs, using slang to talk about what they were taking and expecting to come in. After those kites were intercepted, their rooms were tossed, and each time, they came out empty-handed. We asked if

25

they still had the kites, and of course, they said they were destroyed.

Guard David Chavez was our last interviewee. He did not seem happy about being interviewed, but he basically gave us the same information as the others did. As he got up to leave, Detective Liter put on his "Columbo" hat and said, "One more thing, Mr. Chavez, are you related to CHP Officer Mark Chavez? I know it's a common name, but we are just checking." He then sat back down and said, "Yes, he was my cousin."

He handed us a box of letters that he had confiscated from inmate Cruz that he kept in his locker as he did not trust anyone in the prison, including fellow guards. That was a surprise!

Chapter 12

1975

David Chavez

Mark and I grew up in Los Angeles County, and both attended a private Catholic School, St. Paul High School. We were known on the football team as the hard-hitting Chavez brothers. Of course, we were cousins, but Mark was like a brother to me. I played cornerback on defense, and Mark was our running back. Mark would yell at me during practice, "Hey David, you can't stop me." We had a blast, and we had a good team. Our families were close and never missed a game or scrimmage.

Speaking of scrimmages, our annual scrimmage against Redlands High School was always the kickoff to the season. They had good players and a coach who wore white shoes. Our coach was gruff and wore jeans and a sweatshirt. He was tough but loved us as players. The scrimmage was held at our "house," and it was a brutal matchup. I recall a defensive end and running back named Anthony Garcia, and their quarterback was a top prospect in the nation. We played hard, and I guess you could say it was a draw. We both had great seasons that year, and they were pretty tough for a public school.

Mark said, "That kid running the ball was okay, but not as good as me, HA!" "However, he did give me a good shot while he was on defense, and I was running a sweep." In those days, high school players went both ways: defense and offense.

Mark went on to college, and I got a job with the California Youth Authority as a guard. We lost touch, but I would see him at family gatherings. The last time I saw him, he was going into the California Highway Patrol Academy. We both went our own ways, raising our families.

Chapter 13

2004

Guard David Chavez shared with us how he grew up with his cousin, victim Mark Chavez. Halfway through the conversation, I said I was on the Redlands High School football team in 1975. I didn't remember them as St. Paul played in white uniforms with no names on their jersey, just like Penn State. He remembered me.

"Look, I had nothing to do with these inmates' deaths, and the warden knew about inmate Cruz and my cousin being his victim. I can't say I liked him, but I treated him like all the other killers. You are free to check my locker or my home, for that matter. I have nothing to hide."

We then asked him about the inmates' access to illegal narcotics. He said it's prevalent throughout the prison system, including death row.

"I won't lie, it helps calm 'the beasts."

"What do you do to try and control it?"

"Well, we don't do drug tests if that's your question, but we do "toss" their cells every so often to look for drugs or any homemade weapons."

"Did you ever find any drugs in either of these inmates' cells?"

"No, but we know inmate Cruz was a leader in one of the biggest Hispanic gangs in the state, and we intercepted "kites" and letters to members on the outside regarding drug deals and territories. I'm not sure that has anything to do with his death, but we always felt he got drugs inside as he was connected."

"How could that happen?"

"I'm not sure, but perhaps you should ask his lawyer, as that's the only contact he has with the outside as far as I know." We thanked him and left our card if he had any further information.

After we left, Liter and I agreed that he seemed to be telling the truth. We both agreed we should contact his attorney, but we knew that would go nowhere; it's called "attorney/client privilege." There was one more interview to do, and that was with inmate Josh Wilcox. His cell was between both "victims." He was on death row for the murder of his wife and her brother—a double homicide that took place in the wealthy community of Palo Alto. He was a former CEO of a hedge fund and, according to the guards, a model prisoner.

Inmate Wilcox was escorted in with hands and feet chained to his torso.

"Hello, gentlemen. I wondered when you were going to interview me."

After the introductions, we began questioning Josh.

"I knew both of my neighbors. They both called me 'Richie Rich' after the comic book character. In fact, that was about the extent of their reading—comic books. I'm not sure Jones could even read. We talked about life and how we all grew up. I also helped them with their legal questions, as I am known as the 'death row lawyer.' My nickname is Perry Mason."

"Did you notice anything unusual about the day these two passed away?"

"No, except that they both died on the same day. I found that strange, but of course, no one answers my questions."

"Had they been using drugs?"

"I don't know, but half the time, they were pretty loaded. In fact, inmate Cruz passed his 'samples' around our 'condemned unit' all the time."

"What about you? Do you use?"

"Nope, I'm staying clean as I have a good appeal going as my attorney was incompetent. He was expensive but way too old and fell asleep after his martini lunches. He thought of himself as Clarence Darrow, but he was far from that. Anything else? I know we are all regarded as the worst criminals in the nation, and some of the inmates here are monsters. However, there are some dirty guards in here, and I hope you don't sweep that under the rug."

"Dirty, how?"

"Well, let's just say some turn their heads to things. They also have favorites, like me."

"Isn't that human nature? Well, thank you for your time, and if you remember anything else, let the guards know."

As he walked out, Liter and I looked at each other and questioned the strange exchange. He is a smart killer on death row who acts like he is at a country club. We had to remember that he was a manipulating, sociopathic killer, according to the file we read. The scariest kind of murderer.

Another long day, and it was time to gather documents and head back home. We thanked the warden and headed to our hotel. On the way back, Detective Liter got a call from his partner, Detective Sandy Smith. He put her on speaker as she relayed her message. "Gentlemen, we have fingerprints on the handgun in the Coach Rogers case."

"Well? Do we need a drum roll?"

"Easy Liter, Ha!"

"Travis Williams."

"Any idea where he is now?"

"Last we heard, he was dealing cocaine for the cartel in Miami, Florida."

"EZ, we may be heading to Florida." Well, that's a tough duty. San Francisco then Florida.

After we got off the phone, I told Liter I would start the legal work on my end regarding the death row murders as they followed up on the murder of Coach Rogers.

We had one more Irish Coffee and called it a day. I can say I didn't "leave my heart in San Francisco," but I sure left my wallet!

Chapter 14

1975

The summer before our senior year was so special. Elton John said it perfectly, as we didn't "Let the sun go down on us." We loved the long days, and as Boston sang, "It was more than a feeling." It was magical.

Our band, Mighty Mike, was making some changes to our cover selections after we saw the Doobie Brothers at the Los Angeles Forum. It was a huge inspiration. My girlfriend, Rachel, was working at a local Burger-Taco joint downtown, and the red burritos they sold were amazing. I loved hugging her after she got off work as she smelled like a taco. She hates it when I say that. We were looking for a new bass player in our band as our current bass player was older and had just joined the US Army. I knew my cousin David Garcia was one badass bass player. He was a year younger than me and lived with my aunt and uncle in San Bernardino. He auditioned for us and blew us away. Plus, he was cool and looked like a young Santana. In fact, he brought with him a few of their songs. The music was good, and we played several gigs throughout the summer.

At the same time, I was training for the upcoming football season. There was a group of us that would meet early in the morning to run the bleachers at the University of Redlands stadium. One of those was all-league linebacker Travis Williams, a gifted, fast, and strong friend who had a crazy personality.

"Hey Tony, why am I beating you up the stairs, and you're our running back?"

"I know Travis, you are the man." However, I would always get him on the last interval up these stairs from hell.

Travis loved hanging out with our band and had a thing for Mike Hernandez' girl, Cathy Diaz. "Tony, you think Cathy really is hooked on your lead guitar player? I mean, look at me?"

"Travis, Mike is a good friend, and Cathy is with him like Yoko Ono is with John Lennon, especially in the "Let It Be" album days. She hangs out at our practices all the time."

"Well, she's really cool, and I should be lucky to have her as a friend."

"Yes, you should."

"Tony, I know you're playing at Mike's Fourth of July party. I have some good stuff coming in if you want a kick."

I knew Travis was using some type of "uppers," and I had no desire for any drugs in my system. Well, we did smoke our weed, but I always considered Mother Nature's healthy tobacco. HA! Well, it did make Rocky Road ice cream taste like heaven, and our band sounded better as well. However, I stopped using it as I was getting ready for football, and I wanted a change. Sad to say, Travis got deeper into his drug use.

Travis had a great football season. He led the league in tackles, but we all knew he was high during the games. You could see it in his eyes and how hyper he was pregame. In our first playoff game against one of the Los Angeles Catholic schools, he was blindsided and blew his knee out. It was a tough loss for us but, more importantly, for him, as he had a scholarship to USC pending. This was crushing on so many levels. We all went to see him in the hospital, including Rachel, Mike, and Cathy. Of course, he lit up when he saw Cathy. She just had that personality.

Well, the summer flew by. I will always remember the evenings jumping the fence at the high school swimming pool with Rachel and our friends and hanging out with "primo" Dave and the band. Our best time was playing for our friends and living "life in the fast lane." As I said, it was a "magical mystery tour," and I had no idea where life was taking me, but we took life a day at a time as we danced "in the moonlight," knowing all was good.

Chapter 15

2004

It was great being home for the weekend—soccer, baseball, and a movie—all in that order. Monday came fast. I was up to do my 4:30 a.m. run before the family got up. It was getting cold out, and it hit me. Then it was the first of December, and yes, even in Southern California, it got cold. After my run, I helped with breakfast and getting the grumpy teens ready as Rachel had a job in Diamond Bar as a manager for an insurance company, so she was out the door early.

After making sure my morning duties were done, which included dropping the kiddos off at school, I attended the 7:30 a.m. mass as it really helped me set the tone mentally for the week. This morning, I saw Mrs. Rogers sitting alone. I went and sat by her and prayed as we did the Catholic church's "workout" up, down, kneeling, and sitting. After mass, I gave her a hug and asked if she would like to get a cup of coffee.

"I would love that, Anthony," was her reply.

We went around the corner to my favorite coffee house.

"Anthony, I really miss Greg, but it makes me feel a little better when I see his former players."

"Well, I have an update for you, and it's sad to say that it may involve one of my teammates, Travis Williams."

After giving Mrs. Rogers the information we had gathered up to this point, she promised to keep it confidential as we continued the investigation.

"Anthony, Greg loved all of you, but he always had concerns about Travis, so I'm not surprised."

"What kind of concerns?"

"He felt he was using drugs, and after he caught him selling cocaine that year you were graduating, he told me that he would see Travis off and on years later, and Travis would tell him, 'You destroyed my life.'"

"I had no idea, Mrs. Rogers. Coach should have reported that to his probation officer at the time."

"We had no idea what to do, and you know my husband, he was tough, and I actually felt sorry for him."

"Again, I'm so sorry. We will get justice for Coach Rogers." We hugged, and as I left, I just thought our "motive" got stronger.

As I got to the office, I removed the box of letters and other items from San Quentin and took them up to my desk, where I started to go through all the details. The letters confiscated from inmate Cruz by prison guard David Chavez were full of encrypted information between himself and the Hispanic drug cartel in Southern California. It was obvious he was still running the streets from the inside. After getting help from Liter, who came by the office, we were putting the puzzle pieces together that Cruz was a "boss" in the cartel world, and he had ties across the country and into Mexico. The problem we would have was going to be how to trace these letters. There were no return addresses on those coming in, and he went out to various PO boxes. Most of his letters went out to several PO boxes in the Victorville area of San Bernardino County. Most of the names on the sent letters were coded or aliases such as "Flaco," "Casper," and others with simple initials. However, there was no doubt they were talking about major drug deals. As for the drugs, they were mainly dealing with cocaine. They were talking about "angel powder," "Angie," "California pancakes," and "movie star drug"; that one was pretty obvious. There was the new one we

36

were looking for, "Fentanyl." There were many slang names such as "china girl," "crazy," "dragon's breath," "Fenty fire." It was killing innocent citizens, and now, two of them are on death row.

It was a good thing that I had tried several drug cases in the past. As one drug detective told me, a certain motorcycle gang hates you, as you called them local terrorist drug dealers, in a closing argument. Oh well, I guess I'm doing my job. Along with that, I learned the slang of the drug world. As we finished with the letters, our next step was to call Grover Henry, inmate Cruz' appellate lawyer.

As I dialed the number we had, Liter gave me the look of "Good luck with the shot behind the tree." No kidding. The phone rang once.

"Mr. Henry?"

"Yes, who is this?"

"Anthony Garcia with Detective Dean Liter. We are investigating your client's death."

"Have you ever heard of attorney/client privilege? I have nothing to say, and neither does my client, as he is dead." He then hung up the phone.

"Well, that was a quick interview."

"Yeah, and suspicious."

"Well, Tony, we have more work to do. In the meantime, my team is heading to Miami in our manhunt for Travis Williams."

"It's a good time of year to be in Florida."

"We shall see."

As he was leaving, I said, "Hey, Liter, take your clubs. There is some great golf there." "Tony, you are right. I think you need to come with us in case we need some legal advice or a search warrant."

"Well, that's not a bad idea, let's see how mama will take it."

As he left the office, my phone rang. "Hello?"

"Anthony?"

"Yes."

"It's Warden Godfried. We had another inmate die early this morning."

Chapter 16

As I got off the phone with Warden Godfried, I had two thoughts: one—someone is doing what half our citizens want, a death sentence for the most brutal killers, and two—the media will now explode. It won't only be a page 3 story.

I called Detective Liter right after the call. "Hey Tony, didn't I just see you?"

"Split your team up, part to Miami, and you and I are heading back to San Quentin."

"You got another lead?"

"Nope, another death."

"Oh crap, do we know the inmate?"

"Josh Wilcox." The last inmate we interviewed "Richie Rich." This was not good news as if you believe him, he was not using drugs, so our one theory of self-medicating drug abuse was perhaps out the window. I asked the warden to keep the cell intact. We jumped on a plane the next day, a 6:00 a.m. flight, to get us to the prison by 8:30 a.m.

When we arrived, we got a taxi directly to the prison. We both brought a small bag in case we had to stay over. We arrived at the prison right at 8:30 a.m. Warden Godfried was there to greet us. We had requested ahead of time to interview the guards who were on duty the last forty-eight hours before his death, as well as any preliminary findings on the cause of death.

As we walked into our "workroom," she told us the initial cause of death was a heart attack. It would be some time before we got the toxicology results, but she requested a rush on it. We asked to see his cell before our interviews began. I had Detective Liter take the lead as I was the prosecutor and not the investigator and did not want to become a witness. His cell was just as we saw it before— clean and organized with books piled high from the floor, which included "Helter Skelter" and "The Onion Field."

"Tony, they let them read this on 'the row'?"

"I guess so."

"Tony, check this out."

It was a cell phone that was hidden under his pillow. I guess if he was a model inmate, it appears no one checked his cell.

We then went back to the "work room" and interviewed the five guards who worked his cell unit in the last forty-eight hours. We noted that Guard David Chavez was not one of them.

Guard Tim Johnson, who was first to arrive at the cell of inmate Wilcox, indicated he heard a loud thud and groan. As he approached the cell, he was on the floor. He called for backup and medical staff.

"As I entered the cell, I saw that he was blue in color, and I felt no pulse. The medical team was right behind me and started to give him CPR, to no avail, as he was dead before we even got in his cell."

Like the other guards, he saw nothing unusual before he found him.

As we asked the others, we asked him about the cell phone.

"Well, we try and keep them out of here, but they get smuggled in by family members, and we have caught attorneys handing them out. I guess we screwed up not finding his." After he left, we peeked around the corner to see if the warden was in.

"Come in, fellas. I'm fielding press calls, and if you look out the window, cameras are lined up. We thought that might happen. Do you want to be at the 'press conference' with me?"

"No thanks, we still have work to do.

"Two questions. One, are cell phones a problem?"

"They sure are. Once, we talked about cutting off cellular service to the prison, but the guards' union went nuts as they wouldn't have cell reception as well. So, all we do now is try and keep them off 'the row.'"

"Second, can we have access to the guard's lockers?"

"Yes, they sign a contract that their lockers are part of the workplace. We can search them for workplace issues, and we have, so I'm sure you can in a possible criminal investigation. Would you like to take a look at their lockers now?"

"Yes, please."

"Detective Liter, you have an odd look."

"I think it's time to toss the cells for cell phones, don't you?"

"We are already on it."

A guard then took us to the lockers of the guards we interviewed and guard David Chavez's locker. The assistant warden was there with the keys. After looking into all the lockers, we found nothing that looked unusual except for a cell phone in guard Johnson's locker that was the same model as we found in inmate Wilcox's cell. Liter looked at me and said, "Let's leave it." I knew what he was thinking, "wiretap." Lucky for us, we were alone when we searched the lockers.

As we got back to our workroom, we began the process of trying to open inmate Wilcox's cell phone. As the password block lit up, we tried our first guess, "Richie Rich." Wrong password. Liter said, "Try 'Richie Rich1'. P.O.W.! It opened. There were no text messages, so we then checked incoming and outgoing phone numbers.

"Tony, look at this. His last call was to my phone last night, which I never got."

As I looked closer, he dialed my number but was one digit off. There were several other calls that we would have to follow up on. We then went to his voicemail. He had several from his attorney that we stopped listening to because of attorney/client privilege. The last one took us both by surprise.

"Josh, pick up. I heard what you told that investigator from San Bernardino.

Do not talk to them again unless you want our phone business to end. Don't be stupid, TJ.."

TJ? Guard Tim Johnson? We have his number! It was time to do a search warrant for a wiretap. Liter called his team and said, "Hold off on Miami. We need to tap a phone and have the resources to listen." Detective Smith got right on it and had the on-call judge sign it in two hours. She was good! We were "up" and listening by the end of the day.

We decided it was time to fly back home. We thanked Warden Godfried and told her we were sure we'd see her soon. Thankfully, as we left the prison, all the reporters were gone.

As we flew over the city, it was lit up with Christmas lights, and it reminded me about how many families would have to power through the holidays without their loved ones lost to murder. This case was hard to digest as I can't help but think they (the inmates) got what they deserved. However, I did take an oath of office that I would uphold the Constitution of the United States. It still felt strange, and Dean Liter agreed.

We landed at the Ontario Airport, and I was home in thirty minutes. Rachel was up, and the kiddos were asleep. We caught up on the day, and then she told me not to worry about Christmas shopping as she and her best friend, Kelly, got most of the gifts on "Black Friday," the day after Thanksgiving. That sure helps, I told her. She also said she ran into Christine Stone at our coffee shop earlier today. She was there meeting with several schoolmates from elementary school, a fun group from Oakville. She also said she was heading back to Italy and wanted Rachel to thank me for all I did for her family. That took me back to my early years and the cold case where the silos I grew up around truly went silent.

Time to get some rest, as the next few days will be busy, I'm sure.

Chapter 17

The following day, as I drove to the office, I saw cameras from all over the place outside our offices, including CNN and Fox News. As I parked, reporters started yelling my way.

"Tony, who killed these murderers?"

"Do you have any suspects?"

"We heard there was a third one today?"

I avoided them, and as I entered the office, my boss was waiting for me.

"Good morning, Tony. I'm going to do a press conference shortly. I'm just going to give them the basic general statements about the case and our involvement, but I will let them know it's an ongoing investigation, and we can't make any comments about the case up to this point. They already know who the 'victims' are, as the Warden gave them that information. Would you like to be there with me?"

"No thanks, boss. We have a 'wire' up, and Detective Dean Liter is on his way over with an update."

"Okay! Tony, I'm glad you're on it."

Detective Liter came over with Detective Smith. Both looked like they had just won the Lotto.

"Tony, good morning. Well, guess what?"

"You won the Lotto?"

"You think I would be here if I did?" he snorted. "Guard Johnson got on his phone last night, and we have the conversation on this

44

CD."

"Who is he talking to?"

"Attorney Brad Wilson, inmate Wilcox's appellate lawyer. We know it's him as the number is the same as one of the outgoing numbers of inmate Wilcox."

I sat back in my chair and thought, wow, this will be interesting. I then put the CD into my computer.

"Brad, it's Tim. We have a problem, and I'm not going down for this alone."

"Tim, slow down. What are you talking about?"

"Your client, Josh Wilcox, is dead, but, more importantly, the investigator found his cell phone in his cell."

"He just called me yesterday about getting another shipment of cell phones. What the hell happened?"

"Not sure yet, but I found him dead in his cell, just like the two other inmates."

"Well, let's hope the investigators can't open his phone. That would not be good!"

"It gets even worse. They did a cell search and found twelve more phones."

"Well, I don't see how they could tie it to us. Just lay low, and I'll get back to you."

"Lay low? You still owe me $6,000.00 for the last shipment and distribution of cell phones. I need the money now—for many reasons."

"Okay, I'll come by and will bring the envelope. Stay calm."

I leaned back in my chair and said, "Merry Christmas to me. Well, Liter, good thing we cross-swore Detective Smith."

Liter and Smith were on the Sheriff's plane to do interview number two with prison guard Johnson before I had my second cup of coffee. We only had the "wire" up for so many days, and we wanted to "shake the tree" a little more to get them talking again. Detective Liter was off to interview the other inmates who had cell phones found in their cells.

I'm not sure this phone contraband had anything to do with the murders, but it was interesting that inmate "Richie Rich" had attempted to call Detective Liter the day before he died, a misdial we believed, and was now tied to guard Johnson and his lawyer was involved. This smelled more "fishy" than the Embarcadero in San Francisco, and that could be bad. I then opened my newspaper as I did every morning.

"Who is Killing Death Row Inmates" was the headline on the front page, at the top of the fold. Deputy District Attorney Anthony Garcia was named a special prosecutor in the case. It had my picture staring right back at me. They always use the one where I look tired and angry. Maybe that's how I always look? Oh well, it's on, a true "who dun it?"

Then my phone rang, and it was Mrs. Rogers. She had read the paper and hoped I was still assigned to her husband's murder.

"Mrs. Rogers, I am, and we are continuing to work on the case."

She thanked me and wished me luck on the death row murders but said, "Or maybe not. Do we really care?"

It's what I believe a lot of citizens are feeling. In fact, in the newspaper article, one of the family members of Cathy Diaz, the victim of inmate Jones, said, "I hope he burns in hell; someone is doing what the State won't do."

Chapter 18

"I'm glad we got to use the Sheriff's plane, EZ."

"No kidding, Sandy. The plan is as follows: you'll do the follow-up interview with that crooked guard, Johnson, and I'm going to interview the inmates about where cell phones were found."

"Sounds good."

We landed at the private plane terminal at the Oakland Airport—no fun in San Francisco on this trip. A rental car was waiting for us, and we made it to the prison just after noon. Warden Godfried was there to greet us, and he had set up separate rooms to conduct our interviews. One room was very secure and the size of a cell; it was where I would be interviewing inmates. Sandy got the nicer "digs" to interview Johnson. I was sure her interview would be a lot more fun than mine. Warden Godfried had also told us the results of the toxicology findings for the inmate Wilcox. Not surprisingly, it was a combination of potassium chloride and Fentanyl.

They had a small coffee pot as I sat down in the small conference room. It was just what I needed. As I poured a cup, a guard, Johnson, walked in. It took everything in me to remain professional.

"Mr. Johnson, I'm Detective Sandy Smith; please have a seat."

"Where's the other Detective?"

"He's busy with inmates."

"Oh, I guess you do have to interview everyone as there have now been three murders."

"That's not why I'm here."

"Oh?"

"I want to ask you about the cell phone that was confiscated from inmate Wilcox's cell."

"I already told the other Detective that we missed that one. They are like gold to these inmates."

"What about you? Are they like gold to you as well?"

"What the hell are you insinuating? I don't need this BS. If you have something to ask, then let's get it done—my shift starts in ten minutes."

"Well, let's do that. We have information that you had a little side business on 'the row,' importing cell phones."

"What the hell are you talking about? I'm done here."

As he stood up, I said, "Sit down. I need to play you something."

I opened my laptop and inserted the CD with the recorded conversation over the "wire."

As I played it, he began to sweat, and his face turned flush. I prayed that he wouldn't have a heart attack. He was about three hundred pounds, and I dreaded the idea of performing CPR on this guy.

"Well, what do you have to say for yourself?"

"Do I need an attorney?"

"You're not arrested yet, but I'm sure my partner is corroborating this information as we speak. How did you start this little side business?"

"It wasn't my idea, I swear. Inmate Wilcox comes from a wealthy family. In fact, we called him 'Richie Rich.'"

"So I've heard."

"He was a model inmate but was scared for his life, and he figured out that if he could get phones to the other inmates and do some legal work, that would keep him safe. As you heard on the taped call, his attorney was in on it. We were both making money, and Wilcox felt safe and like a king."

"Well, I guess that didn't work, as he is now dead."

"I don't know anything about that or the other two deaths, I swear! Okay, I did deal illegal cell phones, but that's the extent of it."

"You have two options, Mr. Johnson. One, I arrest you now; or, two, you work with us regarding the true dealer, Attorney Wilson. I can't make you any promises as that's up to the district attorney's office, but we can cross that bridge later."

"I know I'm screwed, but I have a family, and I'm willing to help in any way I can. Are you going to arrest me now?"

"Not yet, but here's how we'll work on this plan. I want you to call Attorney Wilson with a follow-up conversation about your money. Nothing that we talked about. You get that?"

"Yes."

"You are free to go now."

As he walked out the door, he looked like he had been hit by a truck. I also couldn't believe how fast he chose option two. I guess he had no choice.

As I sat in the interview cell drinking coffee from the machine in the paper cups that looked like a deck of cards, I wished I was a part of the other interview, but like the "cold case" involving

50

Christine Stone, I knew Sandy was cooler than I was with hostile witnesses. At least, I thought so.

The first of twelve inmates came in and reeked of tobacco smoke. I guess they got to smoke here as well. Death Row seemed to be more like a country club these days. The first ten I interviewed told me to pound sand, and when I asked about where they got their cell phones from, all ten said to me, "What are you going to do? Give me the death penalty?"

They had a good point. However, the next two were different. One was in for killing her husband and his girlfriend while they were lying in bed, and then she went on to kill the girlfriend's husband. Apparently, they had all been friends. Yikes!

The other was in for a killing spree that involved her boyfriend during bank robberies. Her nickname was "Bonnie," like the infamous "Bonnie and Clyde."

They both had one thing in common other than being murderers. They hated "Richie Rich."

"Inmate Wilcox gave me the phone for a price."

"How much?"

"He was sick. We had to send him nude photos so he could get off."

"You said 'we?'"

"Yeah, me and Margaret, who you are interviewing next. He was a pig; she will tell you the same thing."

And she did. Neither of them knew where he got the phones from, but they both said they were glad he was dead.

Interestingly, the inmates from the female block were forthcoming, and the men were jerks. All in all, I confirmed what we already knew. It was a long day. As we drove back to the airport, Sandy and I shared our information. I, for one, was shocked at how early guard Johnson folded, but then again, it was Detective Smith who did the interview—she was good! We called Tony with the update, and he was pleased with the information we had gathered. We would have to wait to interview Attorney Wilson until after Johnson made contact with him again.

Okay, so we solved a cell phone caper, but who killed these inmates?

Chapter 19

It was Christmas time, and everyone took time off for the last two weeks in December, including yours truly. A week earlier, the Feds (FBI) had taken over the "cell phone caper" as it was discovered that cell phones crossed state lines, and those involved were using the US Mail. Attorney Wilson was indicted along with several guards who were in on the conspiracy. The media called it the "telephone line crime." Some reporters were listening to ELO, I'm sure. Now, it was back to concentrating on the "murders."

Every year, my wife and I throw a huge Christmas party a week before Christmas. This year, we invited friends and family alike, including Detectives Liter and Smith and a new, Spanish-speaking detective who had been recently added to the team, Detective Raul Loftis. He would be an asset when we travel to Miami.

It took Rachel three days of cooking to prepare for the party. Everyone looked forward to the Mexican food that she made, recipes from my grandmother and aunts. Chicken enchiladas, taquitos, barbacoa, homemade rice, beans and salsa, and of course, tamales. The house smelled like a Mexican restaurant for days! I loved it, and I got to be the taster.

The day of the party arrived, and as years passed, it became an "ugly sweater" theme, and of course, Detective Liter wore his ugly "Seahawks" sweater.

It was a full house again, and we played the "white elephant" game and had our annual "couch choir." The choir consisted of the men singing traditional Christmas songs to the wives and kids while sitting and standing around the living room couch. It was like a mini-concert; we all loved it. We entered the room singing "We Wish You a Merry Christmas" and exited with the same song. It was so much fun.

Of course, everyone loved the food and my special holiday martinis, vodka, and cranberry juice. The fellas then sat out back for the special treat—a bottle of "Frank Sinatra," Jack Daniels, and some cigars that I ordered especially for the party. It was at this time that we talked about sports, music, and family. Politics were off-limits!

As we were enjoying our smokes, Detective Liter got a phone call. After the call, he said, "Tony, we need to talk. It was the FBI; one of the guards was "spilling his guts" about the drug cartel and the drugs entering the prison. He indicated that the inmate, "victim" Cruz, was controlling the drugs and his family was part of the cartel from Cuba. Yes, Cuba, not Mexico. All living in… guess where?"

"Miami?"

"Damn, Tony, you are smart."

"Well, let's enjoy the rest of our time off as we are going to be traveling again."

It was time to break out the guitar and strum some Beatles' songs and other classics that everyone knew. I changed the lyrics of "Kansas City" to "I'm going to Miami, Florida, Miami, Florida, here I come." Everyone joined in.

The holidays were always a time to spend with family and friends and to recharge the battery. The whole year was super busy, and I knew 2005 was going to be a big year.

PART II
MIAMI

Chapter 20

1972

It was a very important year in Miami, Florida, as their football team, the Miami Dolphins, won the Superbowl and was the first team in history to go undefeated at 17-0. They were led by the "no-name defense," as they had no familiar superstars on that side of the ball. After the season, everyone knew safety Dick Anderson and linebacker Nick Buoniconti. Their offense was led by quarterback Bob Griese and a tandem of three great running backs: Larry Csonka, Jim Kick, and speedster Mercury Morris. Wide receiver Paul Warfield was one of the best in the league. Head coach Don Shula was smart, tough, and had perfectly coiffed hair. He looked "Miami."

The city was buzzing with excitement—the legal kind, of course.

Miami was also a place where people from the northern coast came to relax and party, especially from the colder state of New York. Others came to retire and start a second business. At the same time, some were tied to the "mob" in New York, the Italian Mafia. One such person was Tony "Fats" Gracciano. He was a big man, around three hundred pounds and only five foot ten inches tall, but very well groomed.

Tony came with a suitcase full of money and opened his restaurant, "Fat Tony's." Yes, that was the name in South Beach. It was located on Ocean Drive, the main street across from the beach, where everyone came to party. The food was actually amazing as he brought his mother from Sicily to be the head chef. The homemade pasta, meatballs, and marinara sauce were to die for. It was served with a drizzle of saffron, the most expensive spice in the world, around the bowl. People from all over the world came to experience this food. One such person was Miguel Cruz, a known member of the Cuban drug cartel. In fact, he moved his family to the United States that year, including his son Richard Cruz, who was thirteen years old at the time.

"Miguel, welcome to my restaurant. Let me introduce you to my head chef, my mama, Camillia."

"Nice to meet you, Senora. I can't wait to try your fabulous pasta!"

Tony's place had a patio overlooking the ocean where they all sat to enjoy a lunch of red wine and rigatoni, served with white mushroom sauce.

"Tony, this is magnificent!"

"Thank you so much."

"Is there somewhere we can talk business privately?"

"Yes, of course, let's go into my office."

We walked to the back of the restaurant, where his office was located. On the way back to his office, I thanked the chef, and she gave me a big smile, not understanding English but appearing to understand my Spanish, "Gracias, muy sabroso."

We entered Tony's office, and it looked like the scene from "The Godfather" where the head of the mafia, actor Marlon Brando, was sitting in his home office at a beautiful desk with leather chairs with dark wood paneling during his daughter's wedding. He poured us both a glass of bourbon "neat" and lit up the Cuban cigars I had brought just for the occasion, and then we discussed business.

"Tony, I'm here to make you an offer. We have worked in the past with our gambling business, and we have developed a great partnership. You are like family. The world is changing, and I know your family does not like the business of drug dealing. The Mexican

Cartel has taken over the West Coast and is trying to move into our territory. I'm not asking you to move any narcotics, but I need a place to launder some money. I'm talking millions. I know you have a gambling parlor in the basement, which I love, and we could move it through the card tables. It's a win-win for both of us. Your cut would be ten percent."

"Well, Miguel, you are right about the drug business. I can't stand it, but money I do like. I can do it, but I want thirty percent."

"You drive a hard bargain. How about I meet you halfway, twenty percent?"

He took a long draw on his cigar, blew out the smoke, stood up, put his hand out, and said, "You have a deal."

I trusted Big Tony, or "Fats" as they called him, and I knew our business was going to take off, and oh, did it!

Chapter 21

1975

Miguel Cruz's illegal empire had expanded in the last three years. He had purchased three car washes, two laundromats (that was appropriate considering what he was washing there), and a hotel, the "M," on Ocean Drive, two doors down from "Fat Tony's." The hotel was amazing, painted bright green and pink—you couldn't miss it. The lobby was decorated with Florida house palms and black and white pictures of famous movie stars who had come to his grand opening, along with "gangsters" from the past. In the corner was a huge floor-to-ceiling humidor with cigars from all over the world. It had a bar inside, and the bartenders were dressed in tuxedos. There was a smaller bar on the third floor, where the pool was located overlooking the beach, with larger palm trees surrounding the deck. It was definitely a 007 "shaken, not stirred" martini place with several cabanas for those who had a little too much sun. Miguel's motto was "live and let die." That would come back to haunt him later.

The Cruz family had moved into a beautiful estate near "Little Havana." Miguel's son, Richard Cruz, had grown up to be a great athlete but secretly wanted to get into his dad's business.

"Pops, I made the All-Star football team as a linebacker last season; it was just announced. I've been invited to the "Top Gun" football camp in Orlando, where players from all over the country come to improve their skills and where college recruiters come out to scout future players."

"Ricky (as his father called him as he was a huge "I Love Lucy" fan), I am so proud of you. This is your chance to shine, and I know your goal is to attend USC in California, but the University of Miami would be a great choice as well."

"I know, Pops, but I would like to go out on my own and see the West Coast and perhaps start a business there or expand ours."

Miguel wasn't sure what he meant by that. *Hotels?*

The camp in Orlando was full of coaches from all over the country. Ricky was with the linebackers, and he met some of the best at his position, including a kid from California, Travis Williams, from some school called Redlands High. They both connected immediately and hung out in the same dorm and spent all day together. The camp was fun, but at times grueling, running and hitting in Florida's hot, humid weather, but they were all treated like high school all-Americans.

When the camp was over, some of the players headed to Disney World. I had been there when it opened in 1971, and Travis had been to Disneyland in California several times, so we decided to blow it off, and I invited him to my house before he flew back to Redlands.

"That sounds great, Ricky. I'll call my mom and let her know. I'm sure it will be fine." And it was fine.

"My dad sent his driver, and he's picking us up in a limo."

"What? I've never been in a limo. Sounds awesome."

The drive back to Miami was beautiful, with blue skies, and the water was an amazing blue-green color, not like the brown water in southern California. The top hit on this date, August 23, was "Get Down Tonight" by KC and the Sunshine Band, and we were blasting it. Windows down and hair blowing without a care in the world. Not yet, anyway. When we pulled up to Ricky's house, I was shocked. It was huge, and it looked like a mansion.

"Welcome to our home, Travis. Ricky has told me all about

you."

"Thank you, Mr. Cruz."

We went upstairs to Ricky's room, and it was huge. The walls were covered with Miami Dolphins photos and posters. One was a picture with Ricky and the Dolphins Linebackers. They were season ticket holders and had access to the Dolphins locker room at times. W.O.W.!

We had two great days at his home and had a great lunch in Little Havana, enjoying a classic Cuban ham and cheese sandwich with a live Cuban band playing Latin standards along with a Santana song every now and then. It was after lunch at the beach that Ricky told me about his family's "evil ways," but he made it sound so exciting. Dealing with cocaine was something I only saw in the movies.

After spending time in the warm water, we headed back to his house. Ricky grabbed a couple of beers from the bar by their pool. We then went up to his Dolphin Shrine. He pulled out what looked like white powder.

"Travis, try this," he said as he pulled out a razor blade and cut the powder into four lines. He then pulled out a twenty dollar bill, rolled it up into a straw, and inhaled. He then handed it to me. I took a hit, and it burned as it went up my nose, but it hit my brain fast. It felt great, and I felt like I could run through a brick wall. Ricky said he did a line before each game. It's not addictive. Little did he know. We stayed up all night listening to Led Zeppelin and Elton John.

The next afternoon, I was going to be driven to the airport. As his dad's driver loaded my suitcase, I thanked my new friend and wished him well on the upcoming football season. We both were looking forward to our senior year and a chance to play in college.

"Travis, here's a little something for you."

It was in a small package wrapped in what looked like tin foil.

"Put it in your suitcase, and don't open it until you get home."

I thanked him and gave him my phone number at home. And as Steely Dan sang, I said, "Ricky, don't lose that number." He laughed, and it was the start of a long-term friendship, or perhaps to call it a partnership would be more appropriate.

Chapter 22

2005

My boss, District Attorney Greg Matthews, was the President of the National District Attorney's Association, and their Spring Board meeting was going to be in Miami Beach, Florida. I was the chair of the Special Circumstance Murder Committee and would be attending as well. The timing was perfect as the homicide team was heading to Miami to follow up on the leads we had regarding both Coach Roger's murder and the Death Row killings.

I was sitting in my office when Detective Liter strolled in.

"EZ, come on in."

"I am in."

"What does EZ mean anyway?"

"I'm laid back and make easy money."

"Well, that's anything but true."

"What's the plan, Tony?"

"Well, it so happens I will be in Miami at the NDAA Conference next week. Can your team be ready to go in a week?"

"We are ready now, Tony."

"Here's what we should do: if you can, go in undercover and try and get rooms at 'The M' hotel in South Beach. The federal attorney gave me some history about 'the row' inmate, Cruz, being tied to the Cartel in Florida. Many of the Cartel members are Spanish speaking, as are the citizens in Miami, so I'm glad Detective Raul Loftis is now part of the team as he is fluent in Spanish. I've had him on past murder trials, and he is great."

"I agree, Tony. I will also split the team up as we have two investigations at once. One is finding Travis Williams, our suspect in your coach's killing, and trying to connect the dots regarding the death row murders. Here is something else we corroborated on a last 'wiretap' conversation regarding the cell phones. In that conversation that guard Johnson had with Attorney Brad Wilson, he made a comment about 'the boys in Miami will not be happy.'

Detective Smith and I then had a visit from one of the FBI agents as guard Johnson was singing like a bird. They are cutting him a deal regarding the cell phones, and he went on to tell them inmate Cruz was the drug dealer inside the prison. He had one visitor who claimed to be an attorney, or at least that was his cover, and guard Johnson would let him in the attorney visiting room with inmate Cruz and not make him sign in. In fact, he knew that drugs were being passed to Cruz, and he would stand guard until the 'meet' was over."

"Really?"

"Yes, the imposter's name was Travis, as he overheard them talking. He would sign in as Doug Smith. The description of Travis matches our suspect to a T. He is Caucasian, around 5'11", shoulder length hair, and, as Johnson put it, has a wild look in his eyes."

"Wow! That is Travis Williams. I still don't understand why Coach was killed."

"One other thing, Tony. We pulled Detective Mike Jones out of retirement to help us with this case. We talked him into leaving his condo in Baja, Mexico, for a few weeks!"

"That's great! The more bodies, the better."

"We will get the team ready to go in the next few days."

"Sounds good. We can meet up at the hotel where our conference is taking place."

"Where's that?"

"The Miami Doral Golf Resort."

"What? Well, we will have a golf meeting for sure."

"Sounds good to me."

"Okay, I'll give you a call when we get everything in place."

"Sounds good. Thank you, Dean."

"Oh, now I'm Dean?"

"HA!"

As Dean Liter left my office, I thought back to my years playing football with Travis and my teammates. *What the hell happened?* Knowing this team of detectives, we would soon find out.

I got home, and Rachel wasn't home from her work commute yet. Meanwhile, Christine and Patrick were starving.

"Hey, Dad, what's for dinner?"

"I think I'll make the best meal in the world for us tonight!"

Pat said, "Oh no, not the hot dog and bean burritos again?"

We all laughed, but they sure were good. The key was to slice up the hot dogs, fry them in a pan, and warm up the Rosarito can of beans while adding sharp cheddar cheese to them. *Delicious!* They both agreed.

Chapter 23

2005

The following day, Sheriff's homicide team 1 was off to Miami, and Detective Liter had a plan.

"Team, let's concentrate on finding Travis Williams first. That may lead us to the cartel and the connections to the prison. Travis is apparently running the drug business in South Beach. The hotel we are staying in is owned by the cartel's boss, Miguel Cruz, and death row inmate Richard Cruz's father. Detective Loftis, that's where your Spanish skills will come in handy. Remember, we are going in undercover as we check into the hotel, but after that, we will need to flash our badges."

The flight to Miami was long, and the layover in Dallas, Texas, wasn't fun. Whoever created a thirty-minute layover should be fired. When we landed in Dallas, we ran like The Beatles in "A Hard Day's Night" to catch our second flight. We arrived at the hotel in South Beach, and it looked like something out of "Alice in Wonderland," but I guess this was the vibe in Miami. The lobby was very clean, with small palm trees all around and framed photos of gangster movies, including a few actors that had stayed there. We checked in under the names of Paul, John, Janice, and George Ramos, brothers and a sister who were here on vacation. We got an odd look as we used the Sheriff's undercover credit card. After we checked in, the plan was to meet at the bar.

The indoor bar was packed, so we decided to hit the pool bar upstairs. It was 7:00 p.m., but the temperature was around 74 degrees. Of course, they sold cigars along with some fabulous drinks. We each ordered a "Cuba libre" rum and coke and grabbed a cigar. We found a table overlooking the ocean as we lit up our smokes. As always, I wondered who owned places like this. Well, I knew the answer in my mind this time: the cartel.

We ordered delicious cheeseburgers as we prepared for the days to come. As we sat there, in walked "the Godfather" himself, Miguel Cruz, with his entourage.

Chapter 24

2005

The NDAA always picked great locations for our conferences. Miami and the Doral Golf and Spa Resort was no exception. As we pulled up to the hotel, there was a huge water fountain that looked like it belonged in Italy. As my boss and I walked in, the staff handed us a glass of delicious water that tasted like a "mojito" without the booze. It was so refreshing. Our rooms were located in Villas named after famous golfers. My room was in the "Bobby Jones" villa with a view of one of the golf courses. This place had seventy-two holes of golf. People from all over the world came to play here. I ordered room service and prepared for my committee meeting scheduled for the next day.

The next morning, I woke up with some very strong and good in-room Cuban coffee. The Cubanos not only roll great cigars, but their coffee is also amazing.

Our committee meeting room was decorated with framed photos of Hall of Fame golfers, and the room was painted gold with white wainscoting surrounding the bottom of the walls. *Was I having a meeting or a wedding? HA!*

My fellow Prosecutors, who were from around the nation and the world, were there. A member from the International Prosecutors Association walked into the room.

"Hey Anthony, how are you? We have been reading about the killings on death row in California, and they picked the right prosecutor for the case."

Deputy DA Marcus Green, from Florida, said, "Yeah, some of our citizens are saying, why can't that happen on our death row?"

"Come on, team, I took an oath of office to seek justice, which means the truth."

"We know, Anthony, but you have to admit it's not your normal murder case."

"That is true."

We had a great meeting discussing cases from across America and a serial killer on the loose in London, England. When our meeting was over, we had a great lunch on the outdoor patio area where the hotel barbequed chicken, hamburgers, and hot dogs!

I would attend other committee meetings as well as the board meeting at the end of the week. When the day ended, I met my boss, DA Mathews, for dinner in the hotel. Of course, it was excellent. We then sat outside for our after-dinner cigar with my best friend, Jack Daniels. The temperature was a nice seventy degrees, and the humidity was low, which made it a perfect setting to sit outdoors.

"Tony, I'm glad we have some alone time this evening."

"Same here, boss."

"I wanted to talk to you about the future of the office. After this term, I am retiring and won't be running for District Attorney again."

I was afraid of what he was about to say and was even more anxious about what came next.

"Tony, I want you to consider running for the position. You have a great reputation and would have the support of law enforcement, victims' rights organizations, and the community, and I would endorse and support you. What are your thoughts?"

"Well, sir, I'm honored and humbled. I would need to talk to

Rachel and my kids."

"I get that, Tony, and I look forward to our next conversation."

As we finished our cigars, I couldn't help thinking about my cases, especially the Coach Rogers murder and the huge Death Row murder investigations. Time was not on my side, as the Rolling Stones sang.

That night, I called Detective Liter. "Liter?"

"Hey Tony, we need to catch up."

"How about golf tomorrow?"

"Well, if you twist my arm."

"I'll get a tee time and get back to you."

"Sounds good." There was nothing better than working on a golf course.

Chapter 25

As I approached the bar, I waved at the table where the boss, Cruz, was sitting.

"Hola, como estas?" Raul was not only fluent in Spanish, but he had great people skills. He could start a conversation with anybody.

"Do I know you?" responded Miguel Cruz.

"No, my friends and I just got in from California, and we are looking for a good spot to have a drink or dinner. I overheard you talking about Fat Tony's. Is that a good place to eat and have a drink?"

"It's the best; the food is to die for, and the chefs are from Italy."

"Well, thank you for the recommendation, and have a good evening."

Detective Loftis was heading back to the table when he suddenly stopped and turned back to the table, rubbing his head, like in "Columbo," the television series.

"One more thing, do you know a Travis Williams?"

Cruz stared at him with a puzzled look. "How do you know Travis?"

"Oh, my good friend played football with him and asked while we were in town if we saw him to say hello. He said he lived here in South Beach."

"Well, he may be around later. He is a manager here and lives in the hotel."

"Great! Thank you, and that cigar sure smells good."

"It's from Cuba. Here, have one."

"Gracias, this is great."

As Detective Loftis returned to our table, he gave us the information he gathered in just a few minutes.

"Are you kidding me?" Detective Liter said. "That's like a hole in one."

Raul said it was his good looks, and the others rolled their eyes. They would lay low tonight and hit Fat Tony's tomorrow. We all went up to our rooms to prepare for a big day tomorrow.

The "Godfather" was about done with his cigar when Travis walked up.

"Travis, my son, how was business today?"

"It's good here in Miami," Travis said, "but the West Coast is drying up. The Mexican Cartel has a strong grip over that region."

"Well, we will see how long that lasts. By the way, a man from California stopped by my table and asked about you. He wanted to say hello to you from a friend you played football with."

"Really, that's odd. Did he leave a name?"

"No, but I'm sure you'll see him here in the next few days. He seemed harmless, but who knows? Should we be concerned, Travis?"

"I don't think so, but I need to talk to you about something that happened in California last year while I was delivering drugs to your son in prison; again, I'm sorry about what happened to him. I took a trip to Southern California, to Redlands where I grew up."

He then told Miguel Cruz what happened regarding the murder of Coach Greg Rogers. "Coach was a good man, and I would never hurt him, but I heard the local police department was looking for me."

"Travis, you better lay low for now; in fact, perhaps head to Key West for a few days. You can stay on my yacht, and we can handle business here for a few days."

As Travis left the table, Miguel turned to his crew.

"I'm still not sure how my son was killed in that prison, and I know Travis would never hurt his best friend."

Of course, Miguel Cruz did not know the cause of death, not yet anyway.

Chapter 26

We got up and headed to lunch at "Fat Tony's." The coffee at the hotel was great, a nice dark Cuban roast that tasted more like an expresso back home. We did a background investigation on owner Tony Gracciano. He had been convicted of tax evasion in New York, and intel said he was tied to the Sicilian Mafia. More importantly, he was good friends with Miguel Cruz; at least, that's what the FBI had shared with us.

"Fat Tony's" was right on Ocean Drive, just a few steps from our hotel. It had an outdoor seating area, and it was a perfect day to sit outside. Fat Tony was sitting inside at his own table in the corner. The tables were covered with red and white checkered tablecloths, and the chairs were dark wood with leather "tuck and roll" upholstery. As he did with other guests, Tony would welcome them into his restaurant with a handshake and a pat on the back.

"Welcome, 'paisanos,' where do you come from?"

"Ciao," said Detective Loftis, "We came all the way from California to try your fabulous food."

"Really? Well, it is a perfect day to sit on the patio and enjoy."

As we sat down, Detective Liter looked at Raul and said, "Ciao, what is that?"

"That's hello in Italian."

"Wow, you speak Italian as well?"

"No, but it's close to Spanish, and it's a beautiful language."

Speaking of beautiful, a waitress came to our table. She had long black hair, big black eyes, and an Italian accent. It felt like we were in Sicily.

After looking at the menu, we decided to share several plates of appetizers—crab cakes, jumbo shrimp "alambre," calamari, and oysters on the half shell. It was absolutely mouth-watering. Detective Jones and Smith went back to the hotel lobby to wait for Travis to come down from his room. We were told he managed the night shift and hit the rack around 8:00 a.m. Time would tell.

Loftis and I stayed and ordered a cigar and an expresso, hoping Fat Tony would come by our table after we lit up. Plus, our waitress was very nice, and I think Loftis had a crush on her. A thought he denied as he had a very beautiful Hispanic wife back at home.

"I'm just teasing you, Raul; she is your type."

"Yours as well, Liter."

Sure enough, as we lit our Cuban cigars, a savory Cohiba, Fat Tony strolled up, and I mean strolled as he was pushing three hundred pounds at least.

"How was lunch? I see you are enjoying our cigars. May I join you?"

"Sure, have a seat."

We shook hands and introduced ourselves using our real names.

"I'm Dean Liter and 'mi chiamo' Raul." The way he rolled his "R" was very cool. We both looked at each other and knew it was time to take action.

"What brings you here other than my fabulous food?"

Detective Liter then went into 'cop mode.' "We are looking for a Miguel Cruz, and we understand that he hangs out here quite a bit."

"Miguel? Yes, he's a friend of mine. Why do you want to find him? Is he in some kind of trouble?"

"We just want to talk to him about his son's death in prison. I'm sure you heard about it."

With that, Dean flashed his badge. "We just want to talk to him about his son."

Tony's eyes bulged as he saw the badge. He took a long drag of his cigar and appeared to be in deep thought. "Well, do you have a card? I will get it to him and have him give you a call."

I handed him a business card.

"That sounds good. Again, thank you for the lunch and cigar."

Tony said, "It's on me."

I said, "Sorry, we can't accept that," and left cash with a big tip. I mean, it wasn't like a free donut—did I just say that? HA! As we left, I turned and saw Fat Tony immediately get on his cell phone.

"Miguel, it's Tony."

"Ciao, Tony. What's up?"

"I just had detectives here from California looking for you."

"Did they say why?"

"Only that it was about Ricky's death, and they wanted to talk to you. They left a card."

"I'll be right over. Maybe it's best I meet them there. I'll bring my 'consigliere'"—his advisor and attorney.

We returned to "The M" and saw Detectives Jones and Smith

talking to the doorman. He told them that Travis left last night for Key West. He was very open after he was shown their badges, as his father and grandfather had been police officers in Florida. We asked him how he left. He said a big black Suburban picked him up around 6:00 a.m. *Damn, I knew I should have gotten up earlier.*

"Did he say where in Key West he was going?"

"He only said he needed some time away and was going out to his boss's yacht, you know, the owner of the hotel, Miguel Cruz."

"You have been very helpful. Your dad and grandfather would be proud."

Well, it looked like it was time for the team to head south. Detectives Jones and Smith would head to Key West, and Raul and I would stay put to contact Miguel Cruz.

Chapter 27

I got on the phone with Anthony, our Tony. I gave him an update, and he thought we were making good progress.

"Thank you, Dean. I can't wait to get our hands on Travis. I have a tee time for us tomorrow, but we can always change it, as I'm here until the end of the week."

"Sounds good."

Around 5:00 p.m., we got a call from Cruz.

"I hear you're looking for me. I'll be at Fat Tony's around 7:00 tonight in his booth in the far corner. I'll see you there." He then hung up.

Well, that was rude, but we will be there.

We headed to the meeting place with the number one goal of finding Travis. We had a game plan. As we walked in, I could swear I could hear the sound of the ocean waves smashing against the front door of the restaurant. It wasn't hurricane season, but the wind was blowing pretty hard.

Fat Tony, Miguel Cruz, and his attorney, "consigliere" Tom Milano, were sipping on a glass of red wine. The bottle in the center of the table was surprisingly a wine from Paso Robles, California, a J. Lohr, not from Italy.

"Gentlemen, have a seat. A glass of wine? Cigar?"

"No, thank you. We are working as we speak."

Miguel looked at Detective Loftis. "Hey, didn't I meet you at the hotel? Did you enjoy the cigar I gave you?" he said with a smirk.

"I sure did, but it kept going out." I wanted to tell him, *"Like you're about to!"*

"How can I help you?"

Detective Liter started, "Mr. Cruz, we want to talk about your son's murder in San Quentin."

"Murder? I was told it was suicide."

"Who told you that?"

"His best friend, Travis. How did he die?"

"It was a drug overdose, but the drugs he took were laced with potassium chloride and Fentanyl, both deadly drugs causing a major heart attack."

Miguel's glass of wine fell over as he raised his hand, pointing his finger at Tom, "I told you something wasn't right!"

"Hold your roll, Miguel," Detective Loftis said. "That's why we are here to help find the killer of your son and the others on death row."

"I don't give a damn about the other killers; I want justice for my son!"

"Calmarse, settle down. We are here as you are the victim's father."

Miguel relaxed as the same waitress we had the day before sprang into action and cleaned up the spilled wine. I looked at Loftis and winked at him; he rolled his eyes.

"Who would want your son dead?" asked Liter.

"I have no idea, but I know he had many enemies."

"Was that because of his business?"

Consigliere Tom said, "Don't answer that."

"Ok, what about Travis Williams?"

"What!? He's like a son to me."

"Well, we know he visited your son at least once a month, and he delivered drugs to him."

"Tom, do you know anything about this?"

"I do not, boss."

"Well, we would like to talk to him. Do you know where we can find him?"

"I already told your partner there that he lives at 'The M,' try there. I'm done here. I have nothing more to say."

As we got up to leave, Detective Loftis did his "Columbo" move again. He turned to the table and said, "Where do you get your cigars? They sure are tasty. Your homeland? How are they delivered?"

"Don't answer, Tony."

"Ok, I was just curious as the DEA just intercepted a shipment of cigars and cocaine in the port of Key West. Apparently, on a yacht called 'The Cruz'. We'll have to check that out."

As we left, I looked at Raul and said, "When did you find that out?"

"Well, Detective Jones used his tech skills to find out the name of his yacht, but other than that, I didn't know anything. I just wanted to see his reaction. Did you see him? He looked like he swallowed a meatball down the wrong pipe."

As we stepped out of the door, the wind and mist from the ocean hit us in the face. A storm was coming, and it wasn't a hurricane!

Miguel got on his phone immediately to Travis, "Travis?"

"Yes, boss."

"Get back here to the hotel as soon as possible. I would've sent our helicopter, but the storm won't allow it."

"What happened? I thought I was supposed to lay low."

"We'll talk when you get back."

I called Detectives Smith and Jones. I gave them an update, and as we were talking, they saw Travis leaving the yacht on his cell phone.

I said, "Green light," and they moved in for the arrest.

"Travis, Sheriff's Department," as they flashed their badges, "You are under arrest."

He looked both ways, but there was nowhere to run except for the water. I hoped he wouldn't choose that route, and he didn't. He was handcuffed and said, "What took you so long?"

We had a long drive back to Miami, and he invoked his Miranda rights regarding the drugs he took into the prison. We didn't mention the murder of Coach Rogers. He looked tired and was as thin as a rail. He did blurt out at one point, "I didn't kill Coach Rogers."

"What? You want to talk?"

"No thanks, but can I have a cigarette?"

"Of course," and Detective Smith obliged.

Detective Liter called Anthony and said, "We need to catch up. I'll see you on the golf course."

"Sounds good, Liter. I'll have the 'smokes' for the round."

Chapter 28

It was a beautiful day with no wind, and the temperature was around eighty degrees. I met Detective Liter at the entrance to the hotel as the Clubhouse was behind the lobby.

"What the hell, Tony? You win the lotto?"

"Take it easy, 'E.Z.,' it's where we had our conference. I'm sure you will know places like this since you were just elected President of the Sheriff's Association, S.E.B.A."

We grabbed our clubs and loaded up for the round, including a couple of Cuban Cohibas. *When in Miami, do like Miami.*

The course was as smooth as a carpet, the fairways were as nice as the greens, and it was wide open with the best kind of trees, Palm trees. We both landed our tee shots down the middle of the fairway, except that Liter's was fifty yards further than mine. Three hours or so in a golf cart gave us a lot of time to catch up.

"I'm going to call you Anthony today, as 'Tony' leaves a bad taste in my mouth."

Detective Liter shared with me for the next few hours what the team had accomplished. I wasn't surprised at all with all they had accomplished over the last forty-eight hours, as they are simply the best homicide team in the country. I had to be careful saying that out loud as I got in trouble at a press conference two years prior. A sheriff from another county got his feelings hurt as they couldn't solve the murder of a family, and our team did. Oh well, I apologized, but I knew I was right. San Bernardino County Sheriff's Deputies are the best!

He briefed me on the arrest of Travis Williams, who was now being held in a jail cell in Miami. His extradition paperwork was filed to get him back to California. After the round, I would contact my secretary and get the criminal complaint ready, charging him with murder, and then I would make a call to Mrs. Rogers.

As we approached the final hole, Liter said, "I heard you may run for District Attorney?"

Wow, word sure gets around fast. "I'm not sure about that yet, as I need to talk to Rachel, of course, and I want to finish both of these cases."

"I get it, but couldn't you do both? Whatever you decide, we have your back."

The last hole was a par 3, 145 yards out over the water. I took out my seven iron and just got over the water. Liter pulled out his nine iron, took a practice swing, and then hit his shot. It was heading right for the flag; it took one bounce and went in—a hole-in-one! He turned back like he always does after a great shot, and we high-fived each other.

I said, "If only our case was that easy, or should I say E.Z. Now I know how you got your nickname."

We had a cold beer at the "19th hole," the outside bar, and developed a plan for moving forward. Who says work doesn't get done on a golf course? I have done my best work playing golf.

After Liter headed back to the team, I made a call to Mrs. Rogers. She broke down in tears and couldn't believe Travis Williams was the suspect, not the defendant. Those were always the tough calls. I was looking forward to getting back home to my office as I had a ton of work to do, and of course, I missed the kiddos. They were growing up fast, and I heard Patrick kicked a 50-yard field goal in spring practice. He had a leg like his mama, strong, not twigs like mine! HA!

The next day, we headed to the airport. Miami Airport was nice and full of different kinds of food choices and pretty cool golf clothing stores. I grabbed a Cuban ham and cheese sandwich on rye, which was delicious, and a diet Coke. I picked up the local paper, the Miami Herald, as I always do in the airports, and the headline on the top of the fold in bold was:

"Suspected Murderer, Travis Williams, from California, a Member of the Cuban Cartel, was Found Dead in His Cell."

What?! I was shocked and wondered why the team hadn't called me, but then I remembered they were in the air heading back home after catching an early flight. The story went on to talk about Travis and his ties to the Cartel and the suspect of a murder in Redlands, California. It indicated it had no information regarding the cause of death. It said he was very close to Miguel Cruz, the boss of the Cartel, and had a picture on page 4 of Miguel with a fat cigar in his hand, smiling like a Cheshire cat. I took a bite of my sandwich and realized I needed to make another call to Mrs. Rogers. I didn't want her to read about it in the paper.

As I got on the plane and took my seat, my phone buzzed. It was a text from Liter, simply, "W.T.F?"

I texted back, "I'll call you when I land."

It was a long flight, and all I could think about was where we should go from here regarding the murders on death row. I had a thought and couldn't wait to run it by the team.

My mind then drifted back to our senior football team in 1975. We had made the playoffs, but we were banged up. Our star quarterback, John, bruised his leg in our last league game, and he was out. Three defensive players were out as well, benched by Coach Rogers. One was our all-league linebacker, Travis Williams. The Saturday after our last game, they decided to make a "beer run," and I mean that literally. They would run into a liquor store, grab a case of beer, and run like hell to get out. Well, this time, they got caught. We lost our game in a tough battle with a Catholic school. If we had our full team, I know we would have won. I now think back on that time as it was the beginning of the end for Travis Williams. I then prayed I made the right choices growing up.

PART III
THE STORM

Chapter 29

2005

Monday morning, on the way into the office, the Doors' "Riders on the Storm" came on the radio. I thought how appropriate it was. I walked into my office to tons of mail and legal motions on my desk after being away for a week. One letter made me smile. It was postmarked from Italy, and the postal stamp had a flower on it.

Dear Anthony,

I pray you are doing ok. I read in the New York Times that I get here on Sundays that you are now part of the team looking into the killings on death row in California. They sure picked the right lawyer.

As you know, Italy banned the death penalty years ago. The Italians are very religious, and the fact that the Vatican is here keeps all Catholics close to their teachings. So, here you are, looked at as a savior. "Saint Anthony," some opposed to the death penalty are calling you. I tell my friends we grew up together.

Our art business has taken off, and Antonio is growing up fast. We are planning to have an art show in New York in the next few years. I hope you can make it.

On a sad note, my mom isn't doing well, and I may be flying back to Oklahoma soon.

"Arrivederci il mio palloncino rosso"—See you soon my red balloon.

Love,

Christine.

Wow, a saint in Italy? That tops it all. Apparently, the deaths on death row were giving a voice to those opposed to the death penalty on an international level, while here in America, it was becoming a political ping-pong ball.

It was nice to hear from Chris, and I will always remember our time growing up and, of course, the cold case trial where we convicted an innocent person for her murder when, in fact, she was alive after being missing for over thirty years. It made me think: one, did Travis Williams kill Coach Rogers? Two, did he have something to do with "the row" killings? And three, if not, well then, who did? About that time, in walked homicide team number one.

"Tony, good morning," said Detective Liter. "We have been working all weekend. We followed up with the Sheriff's office in Miami and confirmed Travis had called Miguel Cruz after they checked their phone system. In fact, it gets better. Detective Loftis has the recording."

My small office was packed, so I said, "Let's go into the conference room."

As we walked over, we all poured ourselves a cup of coffee, Cuban coffee I brought back from the trip, except for Detective Liter, as he doesn't drink coffee. But he can sure put down cokes and donuts! We all sat down, and Detective Loftis hit the play button.

"Miguel, it's Travis. I was just arrested for providing drugs into the prison system. Somehow, they knew I was passing oxycontin to Ricky."

"Yeah, well, I just found out how my son died! He was poisoned by the drugs he was taking. Now, how in the hell did that happen? Did you kill him, Travis?"

89

"Hell no, Mr. Cruz. I would never do that, but there was a prison guard who asked for some pills as well as part of his payment to be our lookout. I swear!"

"Well, if I find out you had anything to do with this, 'Te voy a matar'!"

The line was then cut off.

"Detective Loftis, interpretation please."

"'I'm going to kill you.'"

"Are we sure he hung himself in the cell?"

"We have no other information otherwise."

"Well, if Mr. Cruz is right, our case may be solved or partially solved."

The plan was to go back to San Quentin and take a look at where they store their medicine and who has access, especially the potassium chloride that was part of the "death by injection" protocol.

Secondly, we needed to go back and talk with guard Tim Johnson, who was now trying to save himself with the FBI regarding the "cell phone" case. Was he a killer?

Before we broke up, Detective Loftis made the point that we do know "Ricky" Richard Cruz was considered the main drug trafficker from inside the prison, and the Miami territory was his. Was the motive for Travis to take him out so he could step into his shoes?

"That's a good point, Loftis, but what about victim Doug Jones and inmate Josh Wilcox? How do they tie into this?"

It was a good meeting, but we all felt a political storm was on the horizon. "Well, team, I may call you 'Riders' now."

Liter asked, "What?" I grabbed my guitar I kept in the office and strummed.

There's a killer on the road.

His brain is squirmin like a toad.

Take a long holiday

Let your children play

If you give this man a ride

Sweet family will die

Killer on the Road, yeah

"Jesus, Tony, 'Riders on the Storm,' really? That's creepy, but I have to agree; there is a killer out there."

As the team left, I felt lucky to have them on this case. DA Mathews walked in at that moment.

"Anthony, I just got off the phone with Governor Young. He asked how the case was going, and more importantly, he said he had moved up his plans to close San Quentin."

"What? Where is he going to put all these death row inmates?"

"That's just it. It's the start of his cause to abolish the death penalty in California."

I gave DA Mathews the update but asked him not to share it with anyone, including Governor Paul Young. He understood and thanked me for my work up to this point.

"One more thing, Anthony, have you thought about the DA position yet?"

"Sorry, boss, but I haven't, as I have been swamped, but I will have an answer soon."

"No rush, Anthony."

Well, that was a full day, and I looked forward to getting home. I called home, and Christine answered.

"Hey, Dad."

"Hey Chris, how about 'El Burrito' for dinner?"

"That sounds great."

"OK, I'll be home soon." She was so nice, not to say better than your hot dog and bean burritos.

After getting home with dinner and making sure the kiddos were all good, I sat down and made a strong "Jack" with a splash of coke and shared my day with Rachel. I handed her the letter from Christine, and we were both happy to hear from her. I shared with her that another trip to San Francisco was on the horizon.

"I hope you're getting frequent miles, Anthony, and remember to bring home some of that sourdough bread."

"I sure will."

Chapter 30

Detective Liter and I got another ride on the Sheriff's plane—so much for frequent miles—and Detectives Smith and Loftis went to re-interview prison guard Tim Johnson. As we arrived at the private plane area of the Oakland Airport, there was a driver waiting for us in a black Suburban, courtesy of the Attorney General's Office. As we pulled up to the prison, there were approximately one hundred protestors with various signs saying, "Close San Quentin" and "End the Death Penalty." Thanks, Governor Young, was all I could think of. We met with Warden Godfried along with prison doctor Gordon Frank. We were warned beforehand not to call him Frankenstein, but, of course, Liter couldn't help it. He gave us a look as if we were from another planet. *Way to go, Liter.*

We walked past the empty cells that once held the three dead inmates, and as we moved past other cells, one inmate yelled out, "Hey Tony, who's killing us?"

I turned around, and it was the murderer we had put on death row for killing the family in our local mountains.

We approached a room that had a sign on it that said "Closed." It was the room where the drug supplies were stored for executions. I said, "Closed?"

"Yes," the Warden said, "as we are missing a third part of the drug protocol, the sodium thiopental, an anesthetic."

They still had potassium chloride (that stops the heart and causes death). My next question was obvious, "Is there any potassium chloride missing?"

Warden Godfried looked at Dr. Frank, who said, "Yes, four potassium chloride, 150 mg tablets."

"Four?"

Warden Godfried said, "Yes, and we have not found one in the cells or the yard. Well, not yet, anyway."

"Who has access to this room?"

"Only Dr. Frank and I. Dr. Frank is the one who would complete the drug protocol when a prisoner is put to death."

"What about the regular medications?"

"It's here, off to the right. Clinical staff and guards have access to this room, but the door to the death penalty protocol drugs is always locked or should be."

"What do you mean, should be?"

"Doctor?"

"We found it unlocked after the first inmate death of Doug Jones."

"Did you count the tablets then?"

"No, we had no reason to at the time."

We then left the medical storage area and went back to Warden Godfried's office. Liter and I sat down and shared what we could at the time.

"You can call me Wendy, guys. This has been a tough time. After the cell phone fiasco, I'm not sure how long I will be here. Either way, Governor Young has called for the closure of this place, and I'm not sure where they will house some of the most dangerous here on 'the row' or those with severe mental health issues. I may not be here to see that happen as the Governor wants to see me next week. I don't think it's for a promotion. I do appreciate your work here, but I'm getting blowback from the anti-death penalty folks and letters from others, happy that these killers are dead."

"Wendy, we do appreciate your support and assistance as we continue our investigation." We thanked Wendy and headed back to the airport.

"Tony, for a while there, I thought we solved this crime with Travis Williams passing 'laced drugs,' perhaps with Fentanyl, but the high dosage of potassium chloride and the missing tablets has me rethinking that theory."

"Liter, it sure is intriguing that the drug that caused these deaths is one of the three drugs used in the 'lethal injection' death penalty protocol."

As we got into the Suburban, we told the driver we would get him some lunch at Fisherman's Warf, and he was more than happy to drive us there before the airport. The bread bowl cup of clam chowder was to die for. Of course, my real goal was to get that San Francisco sourdough bread to take home. You know the phrase, "Happy wife, happy life." It's true!

We boarded the plane, bread in hand, and took our seats. The plane is one of those propellor jobs, not a leer jet like the wealthy fly. We had one pilot, and all I could think of was I hope he was healthy. We strapped ourselves in and put our head monitors on, as it was pretty noisy. There was a button to push to have a conversation one-on-one with Liter.

"What are your thoughts, Liter?"

"Well, Tony, it will be interesting to hear what Detectives Smith and Jones get from guard Johnson, if anything. We also need to re-visit guard David Chavez; you know, the guard whose cousin was killed by inmate Cruz. And let's not forget the Cartel."

I looked at Liter and said, "I understand the killing of 'Ricky Cruz' and Doug Jones, but 'Richie Rich' and Josh Wilcox?" That's a wicked curve ball as if 'Fernando Valenzuela' was pitching for the Dodgers. I don't get it."

Liter took his headphones off and motioned me to do the same. He then yelled, "Unless he was about to give up the killer!"

Chapter 31

Detective Loftis and I arrived at the Los Angeles FBI headquarters to interview their "snitch" prison guard, Tim Johnson, who was in their protective witness program at this time. They wanted him away from Northern California. The doors to the lobby were huge, with the FBI logo as big as their egos.

"Good morning, I'm Detective Sandy Smith, and this is my partner, Detective Raul Loftis. We have an appointment to interview Mr. Johnson."

"Come in; we have him ready for you in our conference room. Would you like a cup of coffee or water?"

"Water sounds great, thanks."

As we entered the room, Tim Johnson was there with his new attorney, Tom Murphy. After the introductions, we sat down and got to work. The first thing out of Johnson's mouth was to ask, "Where is that detective with the goatee and the cocky Deputy DA?"

"They are back at your old workplace." Sandy took the lead, and I took notes. "Can I call you Tim?"

"Yeah, sure."

"We have information that not only were you smuggling cell phones into the prison, but you were acting as a lookout when Travis Williams came in to pass items to inmate Richard Cruz."

Johnson looked at his attorney, "Tom?"

"Detectives, is he speaking to you under his ongoing agreement regarding immunity?"

"Yes."

"Ok, Tim, you may answer if you know anything about this."

"Look, I was just there as a lookout. I had no idea what was going on. I did see packages passed, but they put it in a legal-sized envelope like it was from his attorney."

"Didn't Travis Williams sign in as his attorney?"

"Yes, he did, but I never checked his credentials."

"Didn't you think to check the package?"

"No, that's just it; not only was I being paid by the Cartel to 'move' cell phones, but I was also there to help him with any other items."

"Were there drugs being transferred?"

"I never saw them, but I'm sure that's a possibility."

"So, is it possible that Richard 'Ricky' Cruz was the drug dealer inside 'the row'?"

"Not only is it possible, but I also saw him do it."

"Do you know what type of drugs?"

"I do not, but I know they were in a pill form. That's all I know. Look, I screwed up, and I am paying for it, and so is my family. But I will say this: those killers got what they deserved."

"What about inmate Josh Wilcox? Who would want him dead?"

"I have no idea, as he helped everyone with their legal paperwork and gave other inmates hope. He was very bright and came from a well-to-do family. Wait, he was very eager to talk to me about something that came up the day before Cruz died, but I blew him off. He wanted to talk to the Warden, but she's too busy to talk to these killers."

"Ok, any more questions?" his attorney asked.

Detective Loftis then rubbed his head and asked the following, "Did you have access to the medicine room?"

"Yes, I would help distribute the daily meds to the inmates."

"What about the little room that housed the "lethal injection" pharmaceuticals?"

"No sir, that door was always locked. It was taboo to even walk by that small closet of a room. It gave me the creeps."

"Have you ever seen anyone go into that room?"

"Only once, and that was the time that we were about to perform an execution before the Governor stayed the execution of inmate Doug Jones, the serial killer of young women from your county."

"Who was that?"

"Dr. Frank or 'Dr. Frankenstein,' as we called him. He was the one who injected the three-drug protocol, and I think he liked it. A scary dude."

"All right, thank you. We have no further questions, but if you can think of anything else, here is our card."

"Wait, detectives, I heard Travis Williams is dead. Is that true?"

"Yes, apparently, he didn't play his cards right. It's a good thing you are in witness protection now."

As we walked out, we looked at each other and said what we were both thinking. He was right about one thing: the inmates got what they deserved, but Tony was right: we have laws and a justice system that needs to be followed.

On the way back to home base, we were going to stop at Chino State Prison to re-interview prison guard David Chavez, the cousin of the victim CHP Officer whom inmate Cruz had killed. Chavez had transferred from San Quentin to Chino to be closer to his family.

Chino Prison was built in 1941, and boy, did it look like it. There were high fences surrounding the prison yard, but that didn't stop the multiple escapes that had occurred here in the last two decades. One escapee killed a family and is currently sitting on death row. Surrounding the prison are fields of livestock, mostly cows, belonging to the dairy farmers. The aroma was one that stayed with you for a few days.

Meeting us at the gate was prison guard Captain Mike Lemos. After introductions, he said he had grown up in Redlands and went to Redlands High School with Anthony Garcia. He was a very intelligent, "buff" looking guy. He gave us a brief tour of the prison and then had guard Chavez waiting for us in his office.

"What took you so long?"

"Good afternoon, David. Is it ok if we call you David?"

"Yes, of course."

"We just have a few questions."

"That's fine, but like I told the other detective, I had nothing to do with inmate Cruz's death, as much as I'm glad it happened. My cousin, Mark, who he killed, was an awesome person who left a family without a husband and daddy."

100

"We understand and get that. Were you aware of the fact that inmate Cruz was dealing drugs in and out of prison?"

"I heard about his connections to the Cartel in Miami, but if I ever caught him with drugs on 'the row,' I would have busted him immediately! Not that much could be done to a death row inmate, but some privileges would be taken away for sure."

"How well did you know guard Tim Johnson?"

"Honestly, I knew him as a fellow guard, but he was weak. You know, he acted tough, but I could see how the inmates took advantage of him. I'm not surprised he got busted in the cell phone caper. He was used, especially by inmate Ricky Cruz. I once confronted him about that, and his response to me was, 'Cruz is cool,' you want to make some money? I told him to fuck off. He didn't have any idea I was related to inmate Cruz's victim, and I kept it that way."

Detective Loftis then asked him about the clinical storage room where they kept the drugs.

"I knew of the room, but I did not have access to it, as I didn't distribute meds. I hated that role, as I knew inmates were using them to get high or passing them along to other prisoners. I told the Warden as much, but that went nowhere, but at least it took me off the 'candy time' detail."

"Do you have any idea who would want these inmates killed?"

"Half the citizens of the state."

"Well, let me rephrase, anyone inside San Quentin?"

"I have no idea, but I do know this: I left there as 'the row' was not a fun place to work, and it was getting very lax as far as security goes. After all the lawsuits by the anti-death penalty folks and the ACLU, it was getting to be like a college dorm there instead of a prison."

Detective Loftis looked at me, and I shook my head to indicate I had no further questions. We thanked guard Chavez and were escorted out by guard Lemos.

Mike Lemos said, "You know, guard Chavez is one of our best. I hope he helped out." As he opened the gate, he said, "Tell Anthony Garcia I said hello. It's been years, and I married Linda, who went to junior high and high school with us. Also, I know he played football at Redlands and played against all-pro Anthony Munoz. Let him know I run a football camp with him, and I would love for him to come out."

"We sure will, Mike, and thank you for your hospitality. By the way, how do you handle that smell?"

"What smell?"

"Never mind."

Raul and I looked at each other, walking to our car, and we both said, "I guess you get used to it." Mooooo!!

It was time to meet with Tony and give him an update. Just then, Liter called to let us know that Tony would like to meet with the team. He wants to meet at "Muscle Mike's" in Redlands for a beer and an update. Detective Loftis licked his lips and said, "Sounds good to me!"

Muscle Mike's had the coldest beer in town—a "local's" hangout.

Chapter 32

1976 / 2005

As I do at times, I sat in my office, reminiscing about my last year in high school. I loved those days.

It was the bicentennial year, and it just so happened to be our graduation year. Our senior year had been magical, with the exception of losing our playoff game, but as pop's favorite singer said, "That's Life." Springtime in the Redlands was beautiful. The orange tree blossoms were in full bloom, and the homes all over town were sprouting roses. Yes, I noticed that as my grandmothers loved their rose bushes.

My friends were playing baseball or running track, and I loved going to their games. My stepbrother, Sam, was a great center fielder who could run, hit, and catch with the best of them. But the best was going to wrestling matches where a kid named Mike Lemos was an all-league wrestler. As for myself, I got a part-time job at a little neighborhood market, and Rachel was still rolling red burritos.

We loved the weekend parties. I recall hanging out with Richard and, Cathy Diaz and the rest of the gang from Oakville. My brother, Artie, had his own friends, but we would all hang out now and then. I always had my guitar in hand and would break it out every chance I got. "Peter Frampton Live" had just come out, and I learned every one of those songs. But the best parties were the family parties, especially the ones my Aunt Victoria would throw for family and friends. In fact, Rachel and I spent a lot of time at her house on the weekends. To this day, she makes the best homemade tacos ever! She had a huge graduation party for us—I'll get back to that later.

As graduation day approached, we had a full calendar. Final exams, graduation practice, which took place at the "Redlands

Bowl," where graduation was held, and several award banquets. At one of those banquets, Rachel and I were the M.C.'s, and to our surprise, we were voted the "best couple." We were both surprised. What does that mean anyway?

Another fun time was "senior ditch day," where most of us spent the day at Newport Beach. It was a blast—music, firepits, roasting hot dogs, along with a keg of beer in someone's truck.

Until Travis Williams and his crew showed up.

Travis yelled out, "Hey Tony, where's the party tonight? I brought a few of my friends from Miami."

"No party, Travis. We all have to get ready for graduation."

You see, Travis was not graduating with us after Coach Rogers caught him dealing drugs.

"Ok, Tony, well, I guess I'll see you later."

With that, he left. I have always felt bad for him, even then.

My Aunt Vick's party for myself, cousin Zona, cousin Thomas, and Rachel was a blast. She held it the weekend before we walked. The Mexican food was amazing, and cousin Frank was the D.J. playing the best hits from the '60s and '70s. I recall Cathy Diaz was there along with my old bandmates, including cousin Dave. They set up for an evening of live music. They were rocking it, and I actually got to sit in on a song or two. We were all feeling great and excited about the future, but I still had no idea what that meant for me.

Graduation day was exciting and somber at the same time. I knew I would not see some of my classmates ever again. As I walked up to get my diploma, I lucked out as Coach Rogers handed me mine. He shook my hand and said something I'll never forget.

"Anthony, you have the whole world ahead of you. Grab it with all the passion in the universe!"

As I sit here, I can't help but get tears in my eyes. He didn't deserve to die the way he did, especially at the hands of Travis.

That night, we all jumped on buses to Disneyland. That whole trip is a blur to me now, but I know it was fun. The next day, my good friend and star "Q.B." took me to see the "Doobie Brothers" at the Los Angeles Forum. You see, his dad was an NFL Referee and got tickets like this all the time. He went on to Arizona State, and I went my way. We would, years later, catch up when both our sons played football at Redlands East Valley High School. We are friends to this day.

Sometimes I wonder what if I would have met Travis' Cuban friends? I'm sure one was "Ricky" Cruz, as he was called. Could I have changed the direction of their lives by including them in my circle? I guess I'll never know.

Enough reminiscing. It was time to get back to work. I was meeting the team at Muscle Mike's.

Chapter 33

2005

After our "beer meeting," we decided to gather in my office the next day. The Governor was going to have a press conference regarding the closure of San Quentin.

We gathered in the conference room. Detective Smith had brought us all Starbucks and Detective Loftis brought us freshly packed empanada that his wife had made for us. They were delicious!

"Have a seat, team," and as we did, my boss, DA Mathews, walked in.

"Good morning, sir," Detective Liter said, and we followed up with our "Good mornings." DA Mathews then congratulated Detective Liter on his new position as President of the Deputy Sheriff's Association.

"Thank you, sir. I'm not sure what I got myself into, but I'm sure I'll find out soon."

I whispered in his ear, "Do you call everyone, sir?"

"Yes, sir."

Our eyes were then locked onto the TV set. Out walked Governor Young with Warden Wendy Godfried by his side. *WHAT?!!!!!!*

Fellow California citizens and those across our country, thank you for joining me today on the steps of our Capitol.

I first want to acknowledge and thank Warden Wendy Godfried. She has done a tremendous job in these most difficult times.

106

We all know there have been three deaths in the last year at San Quentin, and we continue to investigate them with the help of the San Bernardino County District Attorney's Office and their Sheriff's Department.

However, I'm here today to let you know our plan is to close the doors at San Quentin for good. The prison is antiquated, and it's not a safe place for those who are housed there and those who work there.

Secondly, I am putting a moratorium on the death penalty until further notice.

Warden Godfried will be in charge of the closure and transition of inmates and staff.

Questions?

"Sir, where will you house all the inmates?"

"We will classify them and place them at different sites across the state."

"What about the most dangerous on death row that have mental health issues?"

"Again, we will classify them and put them in the proper environment."

"Do you have a suspect in the killing of the three inmates?"

"That is a question for the District Attorney and the Sheriff's Department. Warden Godfried is working closely with them.

Someone then shouted, "Who needs the death penalty?! Someone is taking care of that for us! Instead of a crime, they should be given a medal!!!"

We all recognized Cathy Diaz's father standing with a group of victims of crime advocates.

The Governor did not respond, thanked everyone, turned, and left back into the Capitol. Warden Godfried looked confused.

DA Mathews stood up and said, "A moratorium?" We were all disappointed but not surprised. "Whether you believe in the death penalty or not," he said, "It is an issue for the voters, not an executive order." He then walked out.

Anthony then turned to the team, "Thoughts?"

To which Liter replied, "Why are we spinning our wheels? Killers are killing the killers!"

"That's just it, Liter, who's the killer? And we do have one totally innocent victim, Mr. Rogers, who, at this point, is not tied to the death row inmates but whose killer may have been deeply involved."

Detective Smith then said, "We all took an oath to follow the Constitution of the State and United States of America."

To which Liter replied, "I know, but I can't help feeling like Mr. Diaz."

"I get that," said Anthony. "What do we have as a team?"

Detective Liter spoke for them. "We have one suspect dead, Travis Williams, who we know killed Coach Rogers, but did he help kill inmate Ricky Cruz? We have two people who had access to the drug potassium chloride. However, Dr. Frank did say the door to the lethal drugs was open at one time. The one I believe had the motive to kill Ricky Cruz was guard David Chavez, of course, but we all believe he is clean, at least at this point. The one that keeps me up at night is guard Tim Johnson. He was part of a criminal conspiracy to distribute cell phones to inmates. He was paid by Brad Wilson, inmate Wilcox's attorney, who was funded by the 'mob' in Miami. He also said Wilcox may have been ready to spill his guts about something. The motive to kill him? And he did distribute the meds to the inmates. Finally, what about Miguel Cruz and the Cartel? I know his son was killed, but we know they were passing drugs onto 'the row' through Travis to his son, Ricky. That smells 'fishier' than the 'wharf in the city.'"

Detective Loftis then raised his hand while rubbing his head, à la "Columbo," "Look, we have several motives for Ricky Cruz being killed, and it appears 'Richie Rich' Wilcox was done in to keep him quiet. What about inmate Doug Jones? How does he fit into all of this, other than being a cold-blooded killer? Tony, what are your thoughts?"

"We may have more than one killer, but I do believe Tim Johnson stands out amongst the crowd. I may have enough evidence to file a case of Murder against him, but it would all be circumstantial," Detective Liter spoke. "We've been down that road before."

Just then, retired Detective Mike Jones walked into the "war room," as I called it.

"Hey, you're not back in Baja, Mexico, yet?"

"Hell no, I never leave a job until it's finished. Sit back and get some popcorn, Tony. I have a video to show you. Remember, you asked me to get footage from any cameras in the areas of the murders? Well, this was the video taken from the 'medicine room' the day before inmate Cruz had his heart attack."

"Are you kidding me?!"

109

Chapter 34

It was good we were in the conference room as he loaded the video onto the new 75-inch monitor. The picture was clear and in color. As he hit play, we all looked on as if we were watching "Star Wars" for the first time, eyes wide open.

In walked guard Tim Johnson, pushing a cart. He walked into the medicine room where the inmates' meds were set up for the morning rounds. After placing the meds on his cart, he turned to walk back out, but then he stopped. He looked both ways and then opened the door to the "lethal drug room," as we now called it.

Anthony told Jones to hit the stop button. Did he use keys? He sure didn't. He just turned the handle and went in. The video continued, and he was in the room for exactly thirty seconds. He then came out looking at his left hand with his palm open and then proceeded to put his hand in his pocket. Again, he looked both ways and then walked out.

Detective Jones then hit pause, and we all looked at each other as if we just caught our man. "Great work, Detective!"

"Hold on, it's not done."

He fast-forwarded the tape, 15 minutes real time he skipped, and another individual entered the picture. *Dr. Frank?!!* The doctor walked into the medicine room and then went to the "lethal drug room. He walked in, and he was in the room for about two minutes. It should be noted there was no camera in the room itself. He walked out and then turned to lock the door. He now had a clipboard in his hand that he was looking at before he walked out. The screen went blank.

Detective Liter said, "Wow, that's like an eagle out of a sand trap!" The other detectives looked at Anthony.

"Well, team, it looks like Tim Johnson is at least our number one suspect, and perhaps it's time to file murder charges, but we still don't have the nexus we need to show direct contact with the inmates."

Detective Smith said, "But Tony, that's just it. He was distributing medications until the day he was arrested." True.

Detective Loftis said, "And the door was open to that room." Hmmmmm, as he rubbed his head. "Any chance we have a video of who unlocked that door?"

Detective Jones said, "We looked, but somehow that part is missing."

Anthony noted that Dr. Frank walking in was disturbing, but he did tell us that prior to the inmates' deaths, he found the "lethal drug room" door open and four missing tablets. The issue now was who unlocked that door?

It was time to visit guard Johnson again. This time, we would read him his Miranda rights, as immunity was out the window. Anthony noted he was going to run it by DA Mathews, but he was ready to charge him with murder.

Before we broke up, we made a call to the FBI agent in charge of the cell phone caper, Agent Steve Hampton.

"Steve, it's Anthony Garcia. We need to interview your informant again, which may possibly lead to an arrest."

"Thanks for the heads up. You are welcome to do it here in our office. Of course, his pain in the ass attorney Tom Murphy will no doubt want to be here."

"No problem. We will see you tomorrow if that works?"

"It sure does, thanks."

After the call, I saw Liter clicking his handcuffs. *Settle down, big boy.*

The nation would be watching all our next moves, I was sure. The Nation? Yes, after that press conference by Governor Young, I was told he was announcing his run for President of the United States. "Riders on the Storm" was stuck in my head again.

Chapter 35

Detectives Liter and Smith decided to make the drive to Los Angeles to arrest former prison guard Tim Johnson. After our meeting the day before, Tony had called his lawyer and told him to have his client pack a toothbrush.

Traffic was a mess on the I-10 West, but it gave Sandy Smith and me a chance to go over all the evidence again. Sandy then said, "Let's stop by Randy's Donuts on the way. I'm craving one."

"Sounds good to me."

"Randy's" was a famous and delicious donut shop with a huge cement donut on its roof.

As we sat and had coffee with our fresh, soft, but crispy maple bar, we talked about how to handle the interview and arrest. We jumped back into our "Crown Vic." We both agreed that a "cage car" was in order.

We arrived at the FBI Headquarters and were greeted by Agent Steve Hampton. We told him what our plans were regarding the arrest, and he understood. As we walked into the interview room, Tim was there with his attorney, Tom Murphy.

Liter took the lead. "Tim Johnson, you are under arrest for the murders on death row. You have your attorney with you, so I don't think I need to read your Miranda rights."

Detective Smith then pulled out her "Miranda card" and read them anyway. That was a good move on her part after thinking about it. Of course, his attorney, Mr. Murphy, said his client had nothing more to say.

"Do you invoke your right to remain silent, Tim?"

He looked at his attorney and said, "I guess so."

"What other evidence do you have?" asked his attorney.

"You will get that discovery soon enough. Let's just say a picture is worth a thousand words, and a video is worth a million."

With that, we had Tim Johnson stand, and I then handcuffed him for the ride back to San Bernardino County. As we walked out, his attorney told him to keep his mouth shut.

We were very professional getting out to the car, and we actually had water for him in the back of our Crown Vic. He looked like he was in shock as he shook his head, talking to himself, or I should say mumbling.

We hit the I-10 East, and traffic was good. On our way back, Detective Smith and I talked about sports, food, and, of course, golf. We didn't say a word about the case.

As we got close to our county jail, Tim Johnson blurted out, "I need to talk to you. I'm not going down for this alone."

We placed him into protective custody and told him he would be arraigned in forty-eight hours. We left and then called Anthony. He's in custody and may want to talk, but we didn't say a word as he invoked his Miranda rights at arrest.

"Great work, team! I'm glad you read him his Miranda rights."

Liter looked at Sandy and mouthed, "Way to go."

"We also got jurisdiction transferred to our county, so we can try the case here. One last thing: DA Mathews has scheduled a press conference for tomorrow morning and would like the team here."

"OK, Tony, I guess I'll have to put a suit on."

"It's not going to kill you," Sandy said. "Plus, I'm tired of those bright green golf shirts you wear." We all laughed.

"Next step, let's follow up with Dr. Frank again. I'm also going to give Warden Godfried a heads-up about the arrest. I'm also sure my boss is calling Governor Young."

As I said that to Liter, DA Mathews walked in and said the Governor would be joining us for the press conference tomorrow; he just asked that we postpone it until the afternoon.

"Well, it's definitely a suit day, Liter, and don't be wearing that funky Seahawks tie."

Anthony got off the phone and called Warden Godfried.

"Thanks for calling me Deputy DA Garcia. I just got a call from the Governor, and I heard about the arrest. Let me know if there is anything else we can do." I thanked the Warden and got off the phone.

We were definitely in "the eye" of the storm now!

Chapter 36

2005–MIAMI

"Miguel, we need to talk. Come by my office. I'll have a fresh cigar waiting for you."

"That sounds great, plus I'm hungry."

Miguel Cruz headed to Fat Tony's. He had read an Associated Press article with the picture of the Governor from California on the front page of the NY Times. Headline—"Death Row Killer Arrested." His plan had worked, at least up to this point.

"Miguel, welcome. Sorry about all these spring break kids, but they do help pay the bills."

Tony had a special lunch of baked rigatoni in rich tomato sauce, stringy, gooey mozzarella cheese, and crumbly beef, combined with perfect al dente pasta in its hearty sauce.

"Tony, this is amazing. I must thank your mama." The cheese was dripping off the fork as Miguel spoke.

After lunch and a nice glass of Italian Chianti or two, they stopped the small talk and discussed the current situation in California. Miguel brought with him two fat Cohibas that they lit up as they sipped on a "Cuba libre" with fresh lime.

"Tony, they arrested 'Baby Hughey' for the murder of my son and the two others in San Quentin." They nicknamed Tim Johnson "Baby Hughey" after the old cartoon for his girth and "weak" ways.

"Finally," said Tony.

"He kept asking for more money from you, didn't he?"

116

"Yes, Travis kept coming back and said 'Baby Hughey' wants more money to keep the cell phones flowing before his arrest and for turning his head to the 'transactions.' He appeared to be getting stressed."

"Did you do in Travis?"

"He did himself in before I got to him."

"Did he kill your son?"

"I don't believe so, but he was starting to lose it. I do believe our plan was going to work after Travis made that huge mistake."

"Tony, well, we thought we had that taken care of; in fact, one of my boys had come down from Sicily to handle it. It's too bad that an innocent man had to go down for it." They sat there with the scent of a mild Cohiba filling the air, and both went over the following in detail to see what, if anything, they missed.

"First, guard Johnson had overheard Travis on several of his visits telling Ricky Cruz he wanted out and was getting help from his high school football coach. He had several conversations with Coach Rogers, and the Coach told him to turn himself in and that he, Coach, would go to the FBI with what was going on in the prison. Ricky tried to talk him out of it and said you owe me!

Second was the debt to Ricky. Travis was in love with Cathy Diaz, who was one of the serial killer Doug Jones's victims. He told Travis he would 'take care' of him inside. Whether that happened or not, we are not sure.

Ricky sent me a message by way of Tim Johnson, 'Baby Hughey,' regarding all of the above. We had to silence Travis and this Coach.

117

The plan was that we 'hit' the coach, take the gun used, and have Travis handle it after the killing; thus, his fingerprints were on it. We took the gun back and told him we needed to grind out the serial number. My guy then planted the gun where it would be found. It was about to work until Travis told a Sheriff's Deputy he needed to talk to the FBI after he was arrested by the detectives from San Bernardino. Thankfully, this deputy was in our pocket. A big dose of Fentanyl and a sheet did the trick."

Miguel then looked at Fat Tony and said, "Add to that, my own son created this mess. First, he kills a CHP Officer that brings the spotlight on 'the family,' and then he tries to take over our business from 'the inside.'" He shook his head as he blew out another puff of smoke.

"What do we do now? They have the weak guard arrested for murder, and I'm sure he will 'talk.' I'm also sure he's in protective custody."

"Fat Tony, we do nothing. There is no way they can tie us to what killed the three inmates, one being my son." With that, he stood and did the Catholic "sign of the cross" on his face and kissed Fat Tony on the cheek as he left.

The mob was alive and well in Miami.

Chapter 37

The press conference went off like they all do, with the Governor sounding like he was giving a political speech about the need to close San Quentin and what he called the "draconian" death penalty. He did give us "props" for how our case was going as we stood behind him and DA Mathews. Of course, Liter wore that horrid green Seattle Seahawks tie.

The press conference ended at 5:00 p.m. with several questions from the media and the public. There were also "shoutouts," one from Mr. Diaz, "Who cares, kill them all!"

Governor Young sped off in his black Suburban to catch his flight from Ontario Airport back to Sacramento.

The arraignment for Tim Johnson would be the following morning. We would all meet in my office and walk over. After saying goodbye to the team, DA Mathews asked if I had a minute, to which I replied, "Of course I do, boss."

We walked into his plush office. I mean, it looked like the Oval Office, with leather chairs, wainscoting, and a beautiful cherrywood desk. Word has it that it cost the county two hundred grand! This, while we all had closet offices and dilapidated carpet. He took a lot of heat over it from both the outside and employees inside, not from me, as he was the boss.

"Anthony, I thought the Governor was over the top."

"I couldn't agree more, boss."

"He is definitely running for President, and he used us for his ambitions. In saying that, I want you to know you have all the resources necessary to finish the job on this case, Anthony." Like my father, he called me by my formal name. It felt good.

"Boss, I don't know what tomorrow will bring, but word is the defendant wants to talk. We also sent Detectives Loftis and Smith to re-interview Dr. Frank."

As I was about ready to leave, he asked again. "Anthony, have you given more thought to the District Attorney position?"

I told him I had talked to Rachel about it on Easter, of all days. "She gave me her blessing to run if that is what I want."

"Great, we need to get moving on that. Do you have a campaign team in mind?"

"No, but I know it will be grassroots. My wife and her best friend, Kelly Collins, will be the co-campaign managers."

"That sounds great, but you will need a good political consultant. I will help you with that."

As I drove home, I started second-guessing myself. I then stopped off at Sacred Heart Church and prayed. I had the church to myself. It was then that I felt I could touch thousands of victims as the elected District Attorney, so the decision was made, thank God, literally!

The next morning, we met in my office with the exception of Loftis and Smith, who were heading back up north to re-interview the doctor. Liter and I headed to the Courthouse. As we approached, there were news cameras squeezed into the courtroom, even the national syndicate, CNC.

The Judge had us first on the calendar to get the "circus" over with. Judge Jim Burr was tough but fair. The defendant was in the holding cell, separated by a glass partition with his attorney, Tom Murphy.

"How do you plead?"

Tim looked at his attorney and then responded, "Not guilty."

Attorney Murphy then made the mistake of asking for a set bail. Judge Burr tapped his wristwatch, which indicated he was not happy, and the attorney was wasting his time. He then turned to me, "Counsel?"

"Your Honor, he is being charged with three counts of murder with the special circumstance of multiple victims. He is actually eligible for the death penalty."

Judge Burr indicated, "Bail denied. Now, let's set the preliminary hearing dates."

"Your honor, we waive a preliminary hearing and would like a continuance before you set trial dates."

"Mr. Prosecutor?"

"That's fine, your honor."

"OK, we will set the next court date 60 days for pre-trial in courtroom number 1. Judge Lisa Warren presiding."

I looked at Liter, and we both smiled. As we were about to leave the courtroom, attorney Murphy approached us and said his client wanted to talk. I just said we would talk soon.

As we left the courthouse, reporters were yelling out questions. One was, "Are you going to seek the death penalty?"

"It's too early for that; plus, it's not just my decision. DA Mathews will make that call."

Then it happened.

"We hear it just might be your call. Aren't you running for DA, Anthony?"

With that, we headed back to my office. Liter looked at me and said, "When were you going to tell me?"

"I was hoping on the golf course."

It was close to lunchtime now, and I decided to dump my PB&J sandwich and get some tacos with Liter. It was "Taco Tuesday." We went to the best Mexican place in town. It was located in the "barrio" across the street from a "Panaderia" that had the best "pan dulce," Mexican bread, in the world.

Detective Liter flashed his badge as peace officers got a discount.

"Something doesn't seem right about that, Liter. No wonder they call you 'E.Z.,' as in, easy money."

"Relax, Tony, lunch is on me, or should I say, the Deputy Sheriff's Association."

Dean Liter was now President Liter. "I'm sure we are going to talk about your DA run and our possible support."

"Possible?"

Liter ordered two steaming hot shredded beef tacos with beans and rice. The refried beans were to die for, and I'm sure they were cooked in lard topped with cheese. I decided to order their delicious chorizo and eggs. The Mexican sausage was spicy and not greasy at all. That, along with a side of "frijoles" and two fresh homemade flour tortillas, had my mouth watering.

We talked about the District Attorney's race that would take place a year from now. We then switched to the case. About that time, his phone rang.

"E.Z., it's Sandy. We just left 'Frankenstein'." Sandy then briefed him about the interview.

"He indicated as he told us before, that he found the 'lethal drug room' door open and locked it. He wasn't sure if he had made a mistake and forgot to lock the door the last time he went into the room. We asked him when that would have been. A week prior to stock, some new drugs arrived. Like all medications, they do have a 'shelf life.' He also had his clipboard that we saw, and that's when he discovered four potassium chloride tablets were missing. Again, it's what he had told us the first time around. As we were leaving, Loftis did his stop-and-pivot move, asking, 'Where do you keep those keys?' Dr. Frank indicated they are kept in his office in his desk drawer. 'Is your desk drawer locked?' 'No, but my office usually is. It's not like the inmates are roaming around'."

After the phone conversation, Liter shared it with Anthony as he was dipping a piece of flour tortilla, like a scoop, into the chorizo.

"Usually," said Anthony. "Usually, I get a royal flush in a video poker game. That's not often. Maybe that place needs to be shut down."

Anthony's phone then rang. It was attorney Tom Murphy asking if he could come by his office the next day. Anthony told him yes, he'd be in the office all day and that he'd have his investigating officer there, and that would be me, Detective Dean Liter. "That was the defendant's lawyer. He wants to talk."

We finished our lunch, and I mean the plates were wiped clean with what remained of my tortilla. On the way back, we both were happy that we were assigned to Judge Lisa Warren's courtroom. She had presided over "Christine's" case. I'll call it that for now. She was a no-nonsense judge. Although the old courthouse would be less than desirable, it would be a good thing to try this case in the winter, if at all possible, to avoid the heat in that department. It was a good day, and we looked forward to what tomorrow would bring.

Chapter 38

The next morning, I stopped into our local coffee shop in Redlands, where our local politicians and community members enjoyed a cup of coffee while discussing local issues.

One good friend held up the newspaper and said, "Good luck, Anthony, I think." Another conservative felt what's all the fuss about those on death row being killed. Of course, everyone in the coffee shop wanted to thank me about Coach Rogers and his killer. I grabbed my coffee to go and headed to the office.

As I walked in, Detective Liter was waiting for me. We were both very interested in what defendant Johnson's attorney had to say. Tom Murphy arrived around 9:00 a.m. after a court appearance. "Good morning, gentlemen."

"Good morning, Tom. Can I offer you some coffee?"

"No, I'm coffeed out. It's been a long day already."

"Well, what do you have for us?" Tom then gave us his pitch.

"We want a deal that you don't seek the death penalty in this case, and we will give you some information on another murder."

Liter and I looked at each other. I told him it was way too early to make a deal, but we were open to it depending on the information.

Tom said, "If it was up to me, I would say forget it, but he wanted me to share the following. First and foremost, he didn't kill anyone."

"Ok, that's what most defendants say, but we can save that argument for the jury."

"Here's what he wants you to know. Coach Rogers was not killed by Travis Williams."

How the hell did he know about Coach Rogers? Tom then gave them both the details about his client being the "lookout" for the Travis Williams and Ricky Cruz transactions and conversations, and how his client overheard the conversation about Travis telling Cruz he was tired of the Cartel and wanted out. He told Cruz that he was talking with his old Coach, Rogers, and he was going to help him. He told Cruz he was the only person he trusted, and they were going to the FBI about the drug trade and the cell phones.

"Coach Rogers told him he would reach out to you, Anthony, to see what steps he should take. However, I know that didn't happen, as he was killed the next morning. How do I know that? My client called Miguel Cruz in Miami and told him everything I just told you. As you know, that is inmate Cruz's father. He told my client, 'No worries, we will take care of it.' Meaning, take care of Coach Rogers. It didn't take long; he was shot dead the next day. Travis never came back to the prison after that, as he knew he was a suspect in Coach Rogers' murder. Little did he know, he was set up. He is willing to testify to this if you cut him a deal."

I looked at Liter and said, "Can you believe this?"

Liter said, "Yes, I always knew there was a connection to the Cartel in Miami. However, I would never have guessed that your coach would be a collateral damage victim to the prison drug transactions."

We thanked Tom and said we would get back to him.

After he left, Liter said, "Now that's a 'curve ball.' Ricky Cruz is dealing from San Quentin, and it makes sense that they have to set up Travis, who was about to go to the FBI, but who killed inmate Cruz, and why?"

126

"I know. This case just got more interesting. Now I wonder, Liter, did Travis kill himself? As for the defendant we now have in custody, here's a motive: inmate Cruz had to go, and so did inmate Wilcox, as they knew too much. I'm not sure about inmate Jones."

Liter said, "I am. Didn't Travis grow up with you and Jones' victim, Cathy Diaz?"

"Yes, why?"

"Jones had to be targeted by Travis through Ricky Cruz."

"Damn, Liter, you are smart! Travis always had a thing for Cathy Diaz. Did he use Ricky Cruz? But how did they get the potassium chloride? All evidence points to defendant Johnson. It's a good thing that the defendant waived time, as we have more work to do. It looks like a Miami Dolphins pre-season game is in order."

We both believed that we had the right person in custody, but did he have help? How do we tie the Cartel into this? At that point, Liter held up his phone. "Wiretap time. Luckily, we have the defendant's cell phone and the prison phone records for a direct line to Miguel Cruz."

Liter called Detective Smith and asked her to start writing up the search warrant for Miguel Cruz's cell phone. Before he got off the phone, he said, "What?" out loud. He hung up and said, "You'll never guess. Travis called Miguel Cruz from a jail phone, the recorded phone. He is not too smart, and that's a good thing."

Chapter 39

2005—MIAMI

"Collect call from the San Bernardino County Jail. Do you accept?"

Miguel thought about it for a second and then said sure. A huge mistake.

"Mr. Cruz, it's Tim. Thanks for taking my call."

"I read about your case. What do you want?"

"Look, they can't prove I killed anyone. As you know, I covered for your son, Ricky. I don't know if he told you, but I also gave him some potassium chloride tablets. I have no idea what he did with them at the time. I did keep one for insurance. And then it happened: inmate Wilcox, 'Richie Rich,' was about to spill his guts regarding the cell phone 'ring' and about Ricky killing inmate Jones. That's when I called you, and you said, 'Take care of it,' so I did. Now, I need your help to hire a good attorney."

"I did appreciate what you did, and Wilcox had it coming. Did you kill my son?"

"Sir, I did not. I know he had many enemies, but it wasn't me. In fact, I helped him with the drugs he wanted to 'take care' of inmate Jones."

"OK, well, keep your mouth shut. We will get you the best attorney out there."

The conversation ended, and that was the last time they would ever talk. Miguel Cruz put a "green light" on guard Johnson, as he wanted him dead. What he didn't realize was that Johnson would now be put in a secret, secured environment after the San Bernardino County detectives heard the above conversation.

Chapter 40

Detective Liter and the team brought the jail recording to Anthony, and after playing it, they all had the same thoughts.

One, defendant Johnson killed inmate Wilcox and may have conspired with inmate Cruz to kill inmate Jones. Two, the "Godfather," Miguel Cruz, was now a primary suspect as a co-conspirator in the "death row" murders.

Anthony then explained that to tie Mr. Cruz to the murders, they would need other evidence. "The legal case is called 'Aranda,' People vs. Aranda says you can't use one defendant's testimony to convict another without corroborating evidence. We need to find other information on the 'Godfather.'" That's what we began to call Miguel Cruz.

"Tony, is all this necessary? They were killers."

"Team, I know, but we must uphold the Constitution, and now we are being used for politics. In fact, the world is watching our case. I got a call and letter from Christine recently, and they are talking about this case in Italy."

Liter said, "It's like being a Seahawk fan. You continue to be supportive even if they can't make the Super Bowl. It's like fighting for losers." We all had a laugh, and I said 2006 might be a good year for you with Matt Hasselber at "Q.B." and wideout Deion Branch is as fast as anyone.

Retired Detective Mike Jones said, "We had the 'wiretap' search warrant signed at midnight by the on-call Judge, and when you are all done talking about football, I have a 'hail Mary' pass for you."

"What are you talking about?"

"Well, the phone call from our defendant to 'the God Father' shook the tree." He then pulled up his laptop. "Here you go."

"Fat Tony, it's Miguel. We have a problem."

"What's that?"

"I just got off the phone with 'Baby Hughey,' and he sounds like he's about to turn into 'rata,' a fat rat! I think he knows about the killing of that Coach, but, more importantly, he may spill his guts about my order to take out that inmate, Wilcox, before he spilled his guts about the cell phones and Ricky's drug connections to us."

"Miguel, we need to stop talking on the phone. Let's meet at my place in one hour. I have a plan."

[The phone clicked off.]

"What the hell?!! There's our evidence. Let's go get 'The Godfather'."

"Hold on, team. Let's see if we can get our current case against defendant Johnson tightened up. I guarantee his current lawyer, Tom Murphy, will have some issues about the jail call and file his frivolous motions, but I want to get him that information sooner rather than later. That may lead to a guilty plea. If not, let's get ready for trial. One thing for sure is we need our defendant in protective custody."

Detective Loftis said, "Already done. I still have friends in the jail. In fact, we are giving the defendant a code name in jail."

"What's that?"

"Seahawk." Liter whipped his head around, and he was a very funny "Raider" fan!

130

On my way home that day, I thought, *what have I gotten myself into? It is a political case that half the citizens of our state say, "Who cares?" about. Also, a case is being used as a political football and, at the same time, planning a District Attorney race. It is very possible that I will be on trial while running a campaign at the same time.*

2006 would be a year that might change my life. I couldn't wait to get home to see Rachel and the kids.

"Hey, Dad, Mom just called, and she's running late. I hope that means your famous burritos?"

"It sure does, Christine. Where is your brother?"

"He's across the street at the middle school kicking footballs."

Of course, he was. He'd been in love with any kind of ball since he was two years old. One other thing that 2006 would bring was that I was going to ask Rachel to retire early or at least work part-time. I needed her, as did the kids, to be closer to home.

As I was frying up the cut hot dogs, Rachel walked in.

"Hey, Tony!" Tony? She called me when she wanted to talk.

"What's up?"

"I'm tired of my commute to Brea, and I got a call from my good friend, Heidi Smalls, at the school district. She said she has an opening for a part-time assistant in her office."

I said, "Let's do it. We can manage, and I'll need you for the campaign, plus the kids will love it!" God answered my prayers, and now 2006 didn't look so bad after all. It was at that time I got a call from Detective Liter.

131

"Dad, it's Dean Liter on the phone."

"Tony, we now know where the fourth potassium chloride tablet is. Warden Godfried called, and we have another death on 'the row.'"

"Who?" I said with a burrito in hand.

"The serial killer who killed over twelve victims that we know of, Bryan McNight, 'the nightwalker.'"

"What the hell?" I said. He was one of the scariest killers on death row, or in the history of California, for that matter.

"Liter, we better get the team together, but it looks like we are going back to your favorite area, '49er's land'."

"Very funny, Tony. I'll see you in the morning."

After I got off the phone, I sat down, and Rachel handed me my "Jack with a splash." I let her know what was happening, and she reminded me that if anyone could handle this, it was me. Then she called me by her nickname, "Mighty Mouse." Hmmmm, "Here I come to save the day!" Time will tell. My drink tasted extra good that night.

PART IV
2006
THE PUZZLE

Chapter 41

The plan was that with little evidence to tie Miguel Cruz to any of the murders, Anthony wanted to solve the murder of his dear friend Coach Rogers.

"I need you and Raul to head back to Miami," he told Liter. "We need to turn Mr. Cruz against Tony Gracciano for the killing of Coach Rogers." Anthony was angry and hurt that his favorite coach was a collateral victim in all this drug dealing and mayhem.

For the last two weeks, the team had been reviewing all the evidence for the killings on Death Row and the killing of Coach Rogers. Anthony had secured an empty office next to his that looked like a war room with witnesses' pictures and statements on the wall and a small model of San Quentin's Death Row on the table that he had the DA's technical staff create. It looked like a model of the "missions" we had to build in middle school. One wall was dedicated to the coach's murder.

Liter looked at Anthony and said, "We got this. We have some intel from our friends at the Miami Police Department about where Miguel Cruz hangs out, and we will definitely need Raul's Spanish skills."

"I'm ready, 'E.Z' Vamos, let's go!"

Anthony said the trial for Johnson would begin soon, and he would be in court while we were in Miami, but that he wanted Detective Liter there. Detective Smith will be his Investigating Officer at this point if the case proceeds to trial.

"Good luck, you two, and, of course, keep me informed of your work down there and have a 'mojito' for me."

"Will do!"

As they left the office, Anthony said, "One more thing, we will follow up on the Death Row 'Night Walker' death when you get back. They are still waiting for lab results."

Loftis and I boarded the long flight to Miami the next morning. We were going to stay at the Radisson hotel in "mid beach" Miami, a mile or so from South Beach and thirty minutes from "Little Havana." We made it to Miami in about eight hours. We had a layover in Dallas, but all the flights were on time.

"Liter, this is a nice hotel."

"Yes, it's dated but very clean and right next to the ocean." The weather outside was a warm 80 degrees but more humid than we ever feel in California. Our plan was to hit "Little Havana" the next morning to confront "The Godfather," Miguel Cruz.

After a good night's rest, Raul and I met in the lobby. The Cuban coffee there was delicious and strong. I was ready to get to work. Raul then walked off the elevator with a Hawaiian shirt on and a white "Fedora" hat. I said, "Really, Raul?"

"Better than your bright green shorts and white 'T,' E.Z." We both had a laugh and caught a taxi to "Little Havana." Neither of us had ever been, but we heard the food and drinks were to die for.

Our friends at Miami P.D. said Miguel Cruz had a daily dominos game at the historical "Domino Park," a place where older Cubans played dominos, but you had to be a citizen of Florida to earn a seat. We were out, but we could watch, of course. The park was located on "Calle Ocho," eight, where all the bars and restaurants were located. We were told Cruz and his entourage usually showed up between noon and 4:00 p.m.

When we arrived by taxi, we could hear live "salsa" music coming from several locations. Across the street from the park was a lively place called "The Ball and Chain." That seemed like the perfect place to wait, and the name could not be better.

"Liter, what do you think?"

"This is great, and I did notice they were rolling hand-made cigars two doors down as well."

The music was playing, and we got a table right in front, which was perfect as the doors were wide open to the street. Imagine a big patio with beautifully painted murals on the walls. It was close to lunchtime, so we each ordered some fish tacos.

"Hey, E.Z., how about one Mojito?"

"I won't tell if you don't."

"Sounds good to me."

"Buenos Dias," said the Cuban waitress.

Raul responded, "Buenos Dias."

"Algo para tomar" (something to drink)," she said.

"Si Senorita, dos Mojitos, por favor.."

"Algo para comer (something to eat)?"

"Si, unos tacos de pescado (fish tacos for both of us), gracias."

As she left to put in our orders, I said to Raul, "Stop staring."

To which Raul replied, "I think she loves me."

"Really, Loftis, Lord."

Our drinks were refreshingly good on this warm, humid day, and the tacos were to die for. Mahi Mahi fish, shredded cabbage, avocado, cilantro, and small pieces of pineapple topped off with a "special sauce." As I bit into one, the flavors exploded in my mouth.

"OMG Raul, these are amazing."

Raul agreed and ordered a side of chicharrónes that came in a little "pig" bowl. "Try these, Liter." They were light, crunchy and delicious.

We had a perfect observation location to watch the comings and goings of the park. So far, no "Godfather." After lunch, we walked over to "La Colada" Coffee Shop, another famous place on "Calle Ocho." We ordered a delicious Cuban expresso. They made them sweet. We then walked over to the cigar shop. We each ordered a beautifully rolled cigar and walked over to "Old's Havana," a Cuban bar and cocina located right next to the park. We got a table out front and "lit up" while sipping the great "Colada" expresso while a beautiful Latin Trio was playing right behind us in the bar. The sound of the Latin beat on the "congas" made me want to dance, but I looked at Raul and said, "Hell no, ha!" That didn't stop Raul from asking the waitress to dance while he was moving his hips to the music, cigar in hand. Just then, we saw the black Suburban roll up. It looked like the President, "P.O.T.U.S.," had arrived. The driver jumped out and opened the door for our man, Cruz.

"Look, Raul, he has the same Fedora as yours."

He was dressed in black slacks, a white short-sleeved button-down shirt, and black loafers. In his hand was a small case that we believed held his dominos. We got information that he played for money, one thousand dollars a game.

"Game on! Let's go."

As Miguel went to the back corner seat, he had two bodyguards with him. Waiting at the table was an older player who looked like an aged "Ricky Ricardo." A full head of hair with a Rolex watch and a huge black onyx ring. Miguel greeted him with a kiss on the cheek. Miguel sat down and then opened his case that exposed these beautiful dominos and two stacks of one-hundred-dollar bills, at least five thousand a bundle.

We walked around the small park, like most tourists, with our heads down, smoking our cigars. Miguel had his back to us as we watched. His guards stood at the entrance of the park. Miguel took out the dominos and scrambled them on the table. He then counted out a few hundred and laid them on the table. Of course, he pulled out a Cuban cigar, and the game was on.

Our plan was to watch for a game or two and then move in to talk to the man.

"Liter, check out the guards. They're harassing the older folks trying to get in here."

Liter said, "Hold on a sec." He then walked over to the two thugs and said, "What's your problem?"

"Who the fuck are you? Go back to your corner with your boyfriend."

As they were talking, Loftis came over, flashed his badge, and said, "You don't want any problems now, do you boys?"

Just then, two Miami Beach Patrol Officers walked up. The timing was perfect, or so I thought. Liter had called them for backup before we went into the park.

"We don't want any problems; we are just waiting for our boss."

"Well then, leave these folks alone and move your fat asses away from the door." Liter was not happy. They complied and walked over to Mr. Cruz.

We walked back in and stood while one leaned down and whispered into his boss' ear. Cruz turned his head around and stood, recognizing Loftis immediately.

"Detective, I didn't know you were a dominos fan. Who's the goatee in the green shorts?"

"Miguel, I'm your worst nightmare. Finish your game so we can talk."

"Give me ten minutes, and we can meet in the bar next door in the back patio area. We can enjoy our cigars there, as well."

We walked back to the bar, and I looked at Liter and said, "Really, your worst nightmare? That's so lame." Liter had to agree, but I could see in his eyes he liked Cruz as much as he liked his "tee shot" into the water.

Cruz and his boys came around the corner, and we followed him to a private table in the back patio area. Liter said, "Have your goons stay back." Cruz nodded to them, and the three of us sat at the table.

The plan was for Detective Loftis to take the lead as they had met before and, more importantly, to treat him like the father of a victim, Ricky Cruz, to get to what we really wanted, "Fat Tony."

Chapter 42

Detective Smith met me in my office as we were going to Department 1 this morning for pre-trial motions in the case of People vs. Tim Johnson. As we were discussing our case against the defendant, my phone rang.

"Deputy DA Garcia, it's Warden Godfried."

"Good morning, Warden. Good timing on the call. We are about ready to head to court on your former guard, Johnson."

"Well, good luck with that. I'm calling to let you know that the autopsy protocol came back on inmate Bryan McNight, "The Night Walker," as well as the toxicology report. There were no drugs found in his system, and he died of natural causes, specifically, a heart attack set off by severe health issues, including being diabetic. He weighed over three hundred pounds."

"Well, that makes our case a little easier as I wasn't sure how or who would have murdered that inmate."

"I thought you would want to know as soon as I found out. The public is still outraged, and we have had daily protestors outside the prison for days. And can you believe this? He had several "pen pals" who they considered to be his girlfriends. A serial killer, for God's sake!"

"Nothing surprises me anymore, Warden."

"Well, I'll let you get back to work. Again, good luck today."

I looked at Detective Smith, and as I told her the news, she looked relieved.

"I can't believe the public supports serial killers, Tony."

"Well, I don't think they support them. They just oppose the death penalty." We then walked over to the Courthouse.

The courtroom was packed with media and the public. As we walked up to the counsel table, we saw the defendant waiting with his attorney, Tom Murphy. It was January, and the courtroom was cool, if not cold. Unlike our last trial, we had in this room in the summer of 2004. That was like a sauna, and I'll take this temperature over the heat any day. From the back of the courtroom, I heard a familiar voice shout out, "Hey, Garcia, why the hell do you care who killed these murderers? They should be given a medal!" It was Mr. Diaz, of course, and I totally understood his feelings. If someone killed my daughter, I would feel the same way.

Defense Attorney Murphy then leaned over. "Anthony, we need to talk. My client wants a deal."

I said, "Let's get through this hearing, and we can set up a time."

"All rise, Superior Court Judge Lisa Warren presiding."

I loved the formality of our court proceedings, as this was where "Justice For All" was served. It was like the feeling I got when I walked into church. As the Judge took her seat, we all sat down.

Judge Warren looked right at me and said, "Counsel, it's good to see you again. How are those little athletic kids of yours?"

"They are not so little anymore, but they are doing great. My son just got a scholarship to Idaho State to kick field goals. He still holds the high school record for a fifty-two-yard field goal. My daughter is now working for the school district and has a deep passion for kids. I'm blessed."

Defense counsel looked at me with that "really?" look, as if I was on my home course. I loved golf analogies. He didn't realize that Judge Warren was tough but fair.

"Are there any motions to be filed at this time?"

"Your honor, the defense has filed a motion to exclude any phone conversations between my client and others while in custody and prior to his arrest."

"Mr. Garcia?"

"Your honor, we have filed our response. Basically, the phone conversations came off the jail logs, which inmates are told will be recorded, and the others are pursuant to a wiretap supported by a search warrant that we submitted."

"Counsel, I will take these under submission. Any other issues?"

We both responded, "Not at this time, your honor."

"OK, the dates on 'the board' are in place (Courts always had the pre-trial, motion, and trial dates on a chalkboard). I will see you in sixty days to proceed with any further pre-trial motions and to begin the selection of a jury. You are excused."

As we left the courtroom, I looked over and saw Mrs. Rogers sitting with her head down. I stopped and said, "It's good to see you. We have some more information on 'Coach's' murder. I will call you later today."

"Thank you, Anthony. I continue to pray for you."

I looked at Smith on the way back to the office. "Something's up if the defendant's attorney wants to talk with us regarding a deal. Let's check on the team in Miami to see how that's going. No word from them yet means they are working hard." To which Smith noted or smoking cigars in Little Havana or both.

As I sat at my desk contemplating our next move, the phone rang. It was Rachel.

"Anthony, don't forget we have our first campaign meeting today at lunchtime in the back room at your favorite coffee shop. Kelly has agreed to be the campaign manager, and I will be the assistant manager. That's how we want it. We need to find a treasurer and a consultant; we can discuss that later."

I said, "Great, I'll see you in thirty minutes."

Kelly was the perfect choice; she was a brilliant small business owner with excellent communication skills and tough nails.

What have I gotten myself into?!

Chapter 43

Miguel Cruz lit up another "short story," Cohiba. I'm guessing he thought he wouldn't be here long. "How can I help you, Detectives?"

Detective Loftis led the conversation as planned. "Miguel, again, condolences on your son's death. No matter what the circumstances, once a son, always a son." As Cruz drew on his cigar, he looked up in the sky and did the "sign of the cross," a true Catholic. They definitely come in all shapes and sizes, and I knew a good one named Anthony.

"I knew my son, Ricky, didn't do drugs. Someone poisoned him inside. And I know that fat guard, 'Baby Hughey,' had something to do with it."

Then came the oldest detective trick in the book. "We have evidence that Guard Johnson carried it out on the order of Tony Gracciano, your Italian friend."

"WTF! Are you kidding me? Why would he do that? There's no way."

"Apparently, Mr. Gracciano thought your son was going to 'run his mouth' about the money laundering going on at 'Fat Tony's.' The defendant confirms this through his attorney."

Miguel Cruz sat there stunned and then looked at Liter. "What do you think, Detective?"

"I think your buddy double-crossed you, but if you help us, we can help you."

"How is that?"

"We also know that Mr. Gracciano put a hit on an innocent

victim. Do you know anything about that?"

"No, and even if I did, I'm not a snitch. I'll take care of Tony G. my own way. Anything else, gentlemen?"

"Not at this time."

As we rose to leave, Detective Loftis made his "Columbo" move again; of course he did. As he scratched his head, he turned to Cruz and said, "One other thing, we heard Ricky was trying to take over the "cartel" business from inside; any truth to that?"

"I don't know what you're talking about, and by the way, the "cartel" is from Mexico, not Cuba. Have a good day, boys."

It was time to call the team and listen in to any other phone conversations that may occur. We also had a craving for Italian food for dinner. "Fat Tony's" here we come. Oh, and we had another plan in mind. However, we needed some help from our F.B.I. partners and their special "Tech" team. They did owe us one for helping with the "cell phone capers."

We had to work fast. Special Agent Jones met us with the microphone and recording device that we would need to monitor. We didn't have the manpower, but we had to give it a shot. We then drove to "Fat Tony's," hoping to beat Miguel Cruz there. And we did.

This time, we asked for a booth indoors, and the waitress took us to our spot. Loftis asked for the corner booth in the back where a reserved sign sat.

"Sorry, gentlemen, that's the owner's booth, and he eats dinner there every night with his special guests." A fact we wanted to confirm. As she left, we knew we might not have a lot of time. Loftis got up to go to the men's room, but on the way, he stuck the little speaker under the table, aka, "007" or "Get Smart," depending on your age.

"Liter, we better blow this place and find a good place to set up shop and listen in if we get lucky." Without saying a word, we got up and left, but damn, the pizza sure smelled good as I saw a customer taking a bit with a string of cheese hanging down her chin like a piece of "silly string."

"Look at that Loftis, 'silly string.'"

"Man, you are old, Liter."

We parked around the corner of Ocean Blvd. and 8th Street by the crowded "Pink Hotel." We had a view of "Fat Tony's," off Beach Blvd., when we walked across the street to the beach access. Not a bad place to wait, and we didn't wait long. The black (P.O.T.U.S.) SUV rolled up with the personal license plate, "El Jefe," which we recognized as Miguel Cruz's immediately. We briskly walked back to our rental car and, with fingers crossed, put our headphones on. We could not be seen from here by Miguel's thugs.

"Welcome back, Mr. Cruz. Mr. Gracciano will be joining you at any time. He has his private booth ready." I followed the hostess back to the red leather, tuck, and rolled booth, and as I sat down, Tony came out with a fat cigar in his mouth.

"Welcome back, Miguel. It's always good to see you."

"Tony, we have a problem. The detectives from California came to see me again, in 'Little Havana,' for that matter. They are on to the plan. In fact, they tried to blame you for the killing of my son, which I knew was B.S. It's a trick they play to pin us against each other."

"Miguel, I would never take your son's life. Why? In fact, I made sure he wouldn't be tied to the drug dealing and any other crimes the other fools were about to spill their guts about."

As he was talking, the waitress brought over a bottle of "red" and poured us two healthy glasses. As she left, Tony went on. "Miguel, we took out that coach to set Travis up and to kill two birds with one stone. I did that on your behalf and your son's."

"Well then, who killed my son?"

"Well, they have 'Baby Hughy' charged, the fat guard, and that makes sense. I think the detectives are here fishing for any more information they can get on him."

"Well, the one detective is not happy about that coach that was killed, and that's what they are looking for."

"Miguel, the person that pulled the trigger is my nephew, Michael Gracciano, my brother's son, who is now in Florence, Italy. They will never find him. You need to stop worrying, and we both just need to lay low for now. On another note, the money flowing through our place has increased. The drug business must be doing well."

"We partnered up with the Mexican Cartel and have more product than we can move. These Americans love their drugs." Our waitress approached again.

Dinner arrived: seafood pasta with fresh clams, shrimp, and a lobster tail on the side. The bread for the table came out steaming hot with a small plate of olive oil and balsamic vinegar.

Fat Tony took a small loaf and dipped it in the tasty oil. As he took a bite, the oil ran down his chin. It was tough watching him eat, and worse was when he talked with food in his mouth. As he

147

was chewing, he mumbled something about the DA in California.

I took my fork and twirled a bit of pasta with a jumbo shrimp on the end. It was amazing, and I wanted to eat as I was not sure I wanted to know about the DA in California. But it didn't matter.

"Miguel, what do you think? Prosecutor Anthony Garcia needs to go."

"What the hell, Tony? That's crossing the line, and they would just replace him anyway." I continued to eat, but now I wondered about "Fat Tony." Was he losing it?

Loftis and I couldn't believe our ears. We both kept looking at each other like we had just won the lotto.

After dinner, Miguel stood up and said, "Tony, we need to be extra careful. Also, never mention the prosecutor again. This is America, not a third-world country. In fact, he is prosecuting the person that killed my son."

"I get that, Miguel; it was just a thought that I would let go. You're right. Let's just sit back and let 'Baby Hughy' take the fall."

With that, Miguel left, and we saw his suburban drive right by us.

"Let's call Anthony," Liter called Anthony and gave him the rundown of the conversation.

Anthony asked, "Did you get consent from Miguel Cruz to record the conversation? If not, it's illegal to covertly place a recording device in a home, office, or restaurant. Although it's inadmissible in a court of law, at least we know we are on the right track. However, we don't have the evidence to move in and arrest at this point. As for the threat to me, it's not the first time. Why don't you pack up and head back home? We need to prepare for defendant Johnson's trial. Oh, and one more thing, get your passports in order as we may be headed to Florence, Italy. I have an International Prosecutors Conference there, and we need to hunt down Coach's killer."

Chapter 44

I was ten minutes late to the coffee shop or our new campaign headquarters. Rachel and Kelly were talking their heads off like they always do. They have been best friends since our high school days when they met working in a taco and burger drive-thru. I loved eating there as their "red burritos" were to die for, plus their drinks came with crushed ice. The best thing in the world after a football practice in the summer.

"Hey, young ladies!"

"You're late, Anthony, but we survived." Kelly had a sheet of paper in front of her with the title in bold letters, "The Plan." I ordered an iced latte, and we got to work.

"The first thing we need to do is hire a campaign consultant. I can manage the team, but I have no experience in 'political mail' or issues to push out, for that matter. Next, we need to start raising money. I have the forms that need to be filed with the State. Third, we need a treasurer, and Tom Marvin has agreed to fill that role. He is a good friend and a retired C.P.A. Finally, Anthony, you need to start getting endorsements."

"I have started that process, and it looks like we will have law enforcement's backing, starting with the Sheriff Association. My good friend, Dean Liter, is the President now. He will help with the other Associations, including some state-wide organizations. It should be a good turnout as we have state-wide positions on the ballot."

"There is also talk that Governor Young is gearing up for a Presidential run," said Kelly.

"I need to stay away from that race," said Anthony, "as I am in the middle of prosecuting the 'death row' murders, and he is now talking about closing San Quentin."

We finished our meeting, and I headed back to the office to prepare for the trial. On the way, I got a call from a possible political consultant.

"Anthony, it's Jack Memphis. I hear you're running for District Attorney."

"That's correct." Jack had been a consultant for several elected officials and was successful.

"Let's meet tomorrow morning," he said. I agreed and gave him the location of the coffee shop in Redlands.

The next morning, we met and had a good conversation about the DA's race. There was a rumor that my former adversary, Public Defender Vance Wright, may get into the race. As we finished our conversation, he looked me straight in the eyes and said, "Anthony, you will never be elected in this County as you're Hispanic."

My brain said, what did you just say, but I stayed cool and only said, "I believe the public is smarter than that." We rose and shook hands, and that was the last I saw of him. You can't have a campaign manager that thinks you lost already. I shared this with Rachel and Kelly. We all agreed to move on as a grassroots campaign. We would cross the campaign manager bridge if anyone else filed for the position. Rachel then pulled out a check. We just got a ten-thousand-dollar check from the Sheriff's Association— we are off and running!

I called Liter and said, "Thank you, Dean."

"What are you talking about?" as he laughed. "There will be more coming. We want to keep people out of the race." As we spoke, he then gave me an update regarding the Miami trip.

"We have our work cut out for us, Dean."

"Yes, we do."

"Golf tomorrow to sort this out?"

"Yes."

The next morning, I woke up with the bold headline—*"**Anthony Garcia to run for DA.**"* It was on for sure now.

Chapter 45

I met with Detectives Liter and Loftis at the Yucaipa Valley Golf Course on Saturday morning. For those of you who say golf is just a sport, I say to them it's also a place where business gets done. This round would be all business.

I drove my "drive" on the first hole into the trees on the left side. Liter said, "I hope we can find that, Tony. That might be harder than solving our Miami case."

Of course, he drove his drive 250 yards down the middle, and he looked back at me with that (Cheshire cat) grin. It was going to be a long round for me shooting an "89", but we got a lot of strategic planning for our upcoming trial and our future plans regarding Miguel Cruz and "Fat Tony Gracciano.

"Tony, we are concerned about the threat we heard regarding you. You need to be careful. We will have our 'Special Security Team' for the Sheriff's Office assigned to you at this time, especially now that you're running for DA."

"Thank you both. Speaking of the campaign, I again want to thank you for your support, but my priority is to hold the killers responsible for the San Quentin murders and Coach Rogers.

"Liter, we talked about going to Florence, Italy, but I'm not sure who we would be looking for."

"I think we start with Gracciano's nephew, Michael, and go from there. When is your International Prosecutor's Association meeting?"

"It's in June, the first week, I believe."

"Well, we will plan on being there."

As we left the 19th hole, the clubhouse, for a beer, Loftis turned to me and said, "Tony, I was thinking about that wiretap we had up on Miguel Cruz and Mr. Gracciano. Is it enough to save that conversation we recorded at 'Fat Tony's'?"

Anthony looked up into the sky and then said, "I think you're on to something here. I will do my research."

I got home and greeted Rachel with, "How would you like to vacation in Europe this summer?'

"Anthony, we can't do that. We have a campaign and, more importantly, our daughter's college graduation."

Darn, she was right again. "You go to your conference, but make it a short trip. I know how important Coach Rogers' murder is to you. I get that."

At that time, Patrick walked in, "Hey, pops, you want to help me kick some field goals at Moore Middle School?" The school was right down the street.

"Of course, son!" and I realized then that I must continue to have balance in my life. As I shagged balls, I couldn't help to feel blessed to have two wonderful kids. We did something right. Just then, I caught one of his 50-yarders on the tip of my index finger. Yikes! That hurt, and it swelled up immediately. It's time for ice and to head home.

Chapter 46

It was now May, and we had trial and motion dates for May 3rd for our case against guard Tim Johnson. The courtroom was packed with both the media and the public alike. The old fans in the courtroom were on, but like in the past, they were blowing hot air. It was going to be a hot day. However, Department 1 was like a museum. I loved the public seating area with the old wooden seats with hat racks, the beautiful counsel table with the wooden spindle bar that separated us from the public, and the huge judicial bench that looked like it was carved out by an artist. It still took my breath away. As Detective Liter and I sat down, the defendant, dressed in a suit, was already at the counsel table, sitting next to his attorney, Tom Murphy. It was at this time that Tom leaned over and said, "Anthony, can we meet in the Judge's chamber before she comes out?"

"What's up, Tom?"

"My client wants a deal, but I want it to be confidential at this time."

I had no problem with this, and I approached the bailiff, Bill Swan, whom I have known for years. "Hey Anthony, are you ready?"

"Actually, Bill, we would like to see the Judge in her chambers."

"Hold on, let me check with her."

He came back out and said, "Gentlemen, come back in." We both rose and followed Bill into her chambers. I asked Detective Liter to join me as well.

"Gentlemen, good morning. Are we ready to proceed? We have a jury panel ordered."

155

"Well, your honor, my client wants a deal."

"What's your offer?"

"To avoid the death penalty, he is willing to plead guilty to the murders of inmate Doug Jones and inmate Josh Wilcox for two consecutive life terms for a total of 50 years to life. He is adamant he had nothing to do with the killing of Richard (Ricky) Cruz."

Judge Warren then looked at me. "Anthony?"

"Your honor, this is all new to me. Can we have some time to consider this plea bargain?"

"I'll give you until the afternoon as you have had months to negotiate, and this should have been discussed before today's proceeding. We are in 'trial mode,' gentlemen."

I couldn't argue with that. We then stepped back out to the counsel table as Judge Warren took the bench.

"All rise, the Honorable Judge Lisa Warren." We then sat back down.

"After talking with counsel, we are continuing this morning's proceeding until tomorrow morning. We will see everyone back in my courtroom at 10:00 a.m." She did not say why, and she left the afternoon open for us to come back.

"Liter, let's head back to the office."

As we walked out, cameras were flashing, and the media was yelling out, "What's happening, Garcia?" Of course, we heard another familiar voice, "Give him a medal for killing my daughter's murderer!"

As we walked back, Liter said, "It looks like we got a 'birdie' on this hole." Another golf analogy, really, Liter?

We went straight to District Attorney Matthew's office.

"Anthony, Dean, come in." We gave him the update, and he asked what we thought. We both felt it was a pretty good offer as we could never prove how he got the potassium chloride to them, but circumstantially, we had a good case, and we both felt ethically he was guilty.

DA Matthews said, "I will leave it up to you, Anthony, but I do know this: the public won't be upset, except for the anti-death penalty folks, but even they will be o.k. with it as we would not be seeking the death penalty as we had decided to do a month ago."

The office had a "death penalty" protocol where the Chief Deputy DA would review the case and a memo written by the trial lawyer. In this case, I had written the memo, and because of his position and the multiple murders, I had recommended the death penalty. It was a split decision by the Chief Deputies, but DA Matthews had the final vote and "green-lighted" the penalty of death.

I looked at Liter on the way back to my office and asked him what he thought.

"Tony, we should take it and run! I don't think he did kill Ricky Cruz as he was scared to death of his father."

"Here's my plan: we accept the offer only if he gives us any other information regarding his role in this mess. If not, we will counter with life without the possibility of parole. Either way, he will die in prison. Let's get some lunch and head back to court."

"Sounds good."

That afternoon, we countered with our offer. The defendant was in the courtroom in a closed session. After his attorney gave him our proposal, he came back to me and said, "He will plead guilty to the two murders, but he has no further information to give you guys."

I looked at him and said, "I'm not sure I believe that. How about this: he pleads guilty, and we come back to sentence him in a month. We take the death penalty off the table, but he earns anything else less than life without parole."

Tom turned to his client, and he shook his head in the affirmative. The plea forms were then filled out, and Judge Warren took the plea.

As I sat there and thought, wow, this could be a book. "Murders on the Row." I kept that to myself for the future.

The next morning, the headline read in bold, "Death Row Killer Pleads Guilty to Killing Two Inmates, but Who Killed Richard Cruz?"

PART V
FLORENCE, ITALY
2006

Chapter 47

Michelle changed her name back to her birth name, Christine, now that she reconnected with her mother, and she no longer needed to hide. She was sitting on her beautiful patio overlooking the Arno River through their beautiful trees and rose garden. They lived on the south bank of the Arno River. The San Niccolo neighborhood was in the upscale part of the city. She and her husband, Francisco, had a very successful art gallery and café located in the "Piazza della Signoria," which was doing great where most of their artwork was displayed and sold.

Two years before, the New York Times magazine had written an article about her "cold case." She was re-reading it and couldn't help but think about Anthony and how hard he fought for her when everyone thought she was killed. She felt somewhat responsible for not contacting Anthony Garcia sooner, but she had no idea a trial was going on about her life being taken in the late '60s. She was proud of Anthony for making sure that the person convicted for her "missing body" case was released from prison. As she was sipping her coffee, her husband Francisco came out to join her with the Sunday New York Times in hand.

"Christine, it looks like your best friend Anthony Garcia did it again, and he's running for District Attorney."

She looked at the headline, "Prison Guard Pleads Guilty to Death Penalty Murders." The article goes on to read the case is not over. It also talked about Anthony's run for District Attorney and what that would mean for the rest of the case and the murder of Coach Rogers.

Christine smiled and said to Francisco, "I think I want to write a book about my case." She showed her husband a small oil painting she had done with the idea of it being the book cover she was thinking about. "Look at this, honey." It was painted in beautiful blue and gold, with a stingray bike, silos, lady justice, and blue flowers in the background.

"Wow, that looks amazing."

"Yes, it brings back memories of my childhood."

"But a novel?"

"Yes, about our childhood and the case. I have read and done my research on the case, and I have a friend in the States that would be my ghostwriter, an attorney now author, Michael Ramos."

"Title?"

"I was thinking about 'Silence in the Silos.'"

"Christine, you are an amazing artist, and I would love to see how you put that creative mind of yours into words." Francisco was always supportive of me. He was ten years older, and I appreciated his wisdom.

The next morning, I drove my son, Antonio, to school on my way to work. Our café, "Expresso Michelangelo," was in the "Piazza della Signoria," a major square in Florence where thousands of tourists and locals loved to visit.

After I put the outdoor tables and chairs in place, I made myself an expresso and sat while breathing in the culture as beautiful doves flew above. Crowds started to gather, and it was time to get to work. As I walked in, one of the young Italian girls I hired said, "Signora, you have a phone call from America."

I asked who it was, and she said, "He told me to tell you it's 'the red balloon.' Do you want me to say you're not here?"

161

"Oh, no, I know who it is."

"Anthony?"

"Christine, how are you?"

"I'm doing great, and congratulations. Francisco pointed out your most recent success in court. We are both proud of you."

"Thank you. I'm calling to let you know the International Prosecutor's Association meeting is going to take place in Florence next week, and I would love to catch up."

"Of course! We can get some fabulous wine and food, and we would love to have you come to our home. Is Rachel coming?"

"No, it will be a fast trip as she is busy with the kids and my campaign."

"I look forward to seeing you, and we do have a lot to catch up on, including a book I may write."

"OK, I'll call you when I get in, and we can plan to meet around my conference meetings. My sheriff detective will also be there on another matter. You met Detective Liter. We are still investigating the murder of Coach Rogers."

"You never stop working, Anthony, but I'm the same way."

Just then, a customer walked in and asked, "How much for your red balloon painting?"

"Hold on, sir, I'll be right with you."

"You painted more of them?"

"No, you have the original my son, Antonio, gave to you, but the

162

prints are flying off the shelves."

"Congratulations! See you next week."

As I got off the phone, my heart was full. Anthony was truly like a long-lost brother to me. He reminded me of the French little boy chasing his best friend, the red balloon, across Paris.

Chapter 48

Los Angeles International Airport was busy, as always. It was decided that Detectives Liter and Loftis would be part of the team to investigate Michael Gracciano and his crew. They had been in contact with the "Polizia Municipale," the local police force that knew Michael Gracciano very well, and they were doing their own investigation at the time. The "Florence Cartel" was running drugs up and down the coast for the Sicilian Cosa Nostra, the Mafia.

Anthony flew out with the team two days before his conference, but he wanted to be there every step of the way.

"Hey, Liter, did you have to wear those green pants and that Seahawks hoodie?"

"I wore it just for you, Tony."

They made plans to stay at a different hotel down the road from the conference site. That made sense. They had also extended a search warrant for Tony Gracciano's phone. The plan was to "shake the tree" to have his nephew call him regarding Coach Rogers.

Our hotel is a small place outside the plaza, and we need to look like tourists. "What's up first?"

"We know where 'Michael G' meets his soldiers. Of course, it's a restaurant called the 'Pegna.' It's full of booths, and our friends at the local police department gave us all the details we would need to have dinner next to them. Perhaps then confront him. Our wiretap should be up."

The flight was twelve hours, with a quick layover at London's Heathrow Airport. Detectives Liter and Loftis headed off to their motel, and I checked into a very nice hotel, "In Piazza della Signoria," located on the Square of Signoria. The International

Prosecutor's Association always picked some amazing places to hold their annual conference. The hotel was beautifully decorated. The room was charming, decorated with fanciful frescoes paintings on the plaster itself, with a view of the Plaza. After I settled in, I called Rachel to let her know I had made it safe, and then I called Christine to set up our lunch. My phone then rang, and it was Liter.

"Tony, we are in, and our plan is to make contact with Michael G. tonight. Detective Smith said our wire is up and running on 'Tony G's' phone."

"You two work fast. Call me, or better yet, let's meet tomorrow at this great café I know of."

"Oh, you mean your old girlfriends? Ha!" was Liter's reply.

"Very funny, Dean."

I met Christine at the café she named "Michelle's" after she had changed her name. As I walked up, out walked the girl with the big hair. "Anthony! Welcome to my second home."

"Chris, you look great. It's so good to see you again."

"Yeah, after your trial where I was missing, I decided to take my name back. My son was a little confused at first, but I explained, and he now gets it. Let me show you my place, and then we can sit at my favorite table out here on the Piazza. Come on in, Anthony. As you can see, my place is also my art center." Her beautiful oil paintings covered the walls with various prices in the lower corners of the pieces. "I love Italy, as you can see, as ninety percent of my work captures the beauty of my new country. You know I became an Italian citizen after I moved here with Francisco."

"I thought you might have."

165

At that moment, a beautiful picture caught my eye. It was the little French boy from our favorite movie being carried up into the sky with a multi-colored spray of balloons. The price was 470.00 euros. $500.00 in our greenbacks. "I love that, but it may be outside my budget."

"We can work on that, Anthony." I marveled at how beautiful a Euro was to our boring green money. It was like art itself.

"This is our coffee and expresso counter, and just to the left is our lunch menu, which we keep on a chalkboard as it changes daily. Oh, and the wine menu is here as well." She pointed to an empty wine bottle with a list of wines painted on by a small paintbrush in white.

"I'm going to order a summer dish. Tuscan bread combined with tomatoes, cucumber, and basil soaked with Tuscan olive oil and a glass of our famous Libero Chianti."

"That sounds wonderful." We proceeded outside to our corner, where white and red checkered tablecloths covered the table overlooking the most beautiful Piazza ever.

"It's so nice to see you, Anthony. How is the family?"

"We are doing well, Christine. My daughter and Patrick are the best kids ever. It is interesting how my daughter was named after you, of course, when I thought you were gone. She also has the middle name of Michele, with one "L," and you changed your name to that in real life, and you named this beautiful café the same. Rachel is working hard and is now working on my campaign for District Attorney. We are super busy, but good. How about you?"

"Francisco has done an amazing job as our bookkeeper for our café and my paint sales, and he now teaches art at the Mandragora Art Store. Antonio is a wonderful little boy. He loves school, and is

166

a good little futbol player, soccer in America. And he wants to be an "Arrocato," an attorney when he grows up, and specifically an "Il procurator," a prosecuting attorney. Can you believe that?! He said just like my American friend."

We sat catching up about life and work. Her art has been selling faster than she can paint, and now she sells original copies across Italy. "My next goal, Anthony, is an art show in New York."

"That would be amazing, Chris."

The food was amazing, and after lunch, we had an Italian coffee that was like an expresso in the U.S. I couldn't help but say a prayer as we sat looking at the beautiful, rich, artistic church across the way.

"I best get on my way. I'm meeting some other prosecutors from Italy to go over our agenda, and I'm meeting with my detectives."

"It was so nice to see you, Anthony. Let's have dinner at my home before you leave."

"I would love that." As I walked away, I thanked God for how her life turned out. I can't wait to share that with my cousin Zona, who was her best friend in elementary school.

Chapter 49

Detective Loftis and I entered the "ristorante" at the time our Italian police officers told us Michael Gracciano would be there, and there he was in a corner booth holding court.

"Let's try to get the booth next to theirs, Raul."

"That sounds like a plan." The hostess came over, and we asked for the booth we wanted. As she walked us to our location, Michael turned and looked at us and said, "American Seahawk fan, really?"

"What's that?" asked one of his thugs.

"It's a football team in America that passes when they should run."

I looked at Raul and said, "At least he knows his football."

"And high school football coaches," he said under his breath.

Of course, our waitress was a beautiful, dark-haired Italian girl who spoke little, if any, English. Raul was staring so hard that he almost scared her away. That was when I called him by his last name, "Easy Loftis."

"No, you're 'E.Z,' Liter."

With some help from Loftis, we were able to order two cold beers and a pizza. As we waited for our order, we tried to listen to the conversation in the next booth. We could pick up bits and pieces of the "Cartel Board Meeting":

Michael, it's getting worse on the streets. The Mexican Cartel is moving in, and they are ruthless with no sense of respect.

Are they here in Florence?

Yes, a small group from Miami where they are at war with "Don Graccinos'" friend, Miguel Cruz.

Well, let's put an end to it sooner than later. Get our soldiers ready. We will scatter them like the cockroaches they are.

Our pizza came just as the fools next to us switched their conversation to futbol.

"Liter, they speak pretty good English."

"Of course they do. They live part of their lives in America."

We ordered another ice-cold "Peroni" as our pizza arrived. The pizza was amazing. The pepperoni was curled up at its edges, slightly burned, and the mozzarella cheese was to die for. We both dug in, not realizing how hungry we were. The plan was to finish lunch and wait for Michael to make his move and then "shake the tree," knowing he would call his "Zio," his uncle after we confronted him. We were about done when his "crew" stood up, getting ready to leave. It was time to move in.

"Mr. Gracciano, Detective Liter from America," as I flashed my badge, "and my partner, Raul Loftis. We need a few minutes of your time."

"Do you have jurisdiction here?"

"Yes, we do, as we are investigating a murder that occurred in California." We then pulled the old investigator's trick, and we lied. "We found your fingerprint on the murder weapon, a gun!"

"You have the wrong guy."

"Isn't your uncle Tony Gracciano?"

"Yeah, so what?"

"Why don't we have a seat, and we can talk."

"I have nothing to say to you. I have never been to California, and unless you're going to arrest me, have a nice day." He turned and walked away.

"That should do it, Liter. I'll call Detectives Smith and Jones and tell them to start monitoring 'Fat Tony's' cell."

"Well, let's wait until morning to call, as it is 2:00 a.m. at home."

The following day, Detective Liter's phone rang. "Good morning, Dean. We waited to call you as you need your beauty sleep."

"Thanks. I was going to call you yesterday, but it was 2:00 a.m. for you."

"Detective Jones and I have something you'll want to hear. Whatever you said to Mr. Gracciano worked."

As I sipped my strong Italian coffee, I said, "Let's hear what you got."

"Good morning, Dean, it's Mike. I'll key it up now, but after this, can I go back to my retirement condo in Baja?"

"Maybe we may need you for court soon, according to Anthony."

I sat back and put my phone on speaker mode. Tony Gracciano's phone rang at 6:00 a.m.:

Don Gracciano, Good morning.

Michael? How could I know if it's good or not? It's early here in Miami.

I know, but I had to get a hold of you. I just left dinner, and two Detectives from California approached me and were "busting my balls" about the murder of that witness in Redlands. They said they had my fingerprints on the handgun I used, but that would be impossible as I used gloves.

The other end got silent for a few seconds. Guard "Baby Hughey" must be talking. We better take care of him. He then heard some static on the phone.

Michael, we need to get off the phone. Get on a plane to Miami as soon as you can. Plus, we have other business to discuss.

I'll see you tomorrow, Don Gracciano.

The phone then went silent.

"Another 'hole in one' team. I'll get this information to Anthony and decide where we want to arrest him. If we get him in the States, it may be less of a hassle regarding extradition."

"Anthony, good morning or 'Buongiorno' as they say here."

"Ciao", that's hello, Liter."

"I know! Let's get an expresso."

"Perfect, grab Detective Loftis, and I'll meet you at "Michelle's Café."

"Perfect."

We met an hour later, and Christine greeted us with open arms. She had met Dean Liter from our missing persons case, and I introduced her to Detective Raul Loftis. We sat at an outdoor table, and she brought us our coffee and some delicious pastries. I'm sure to gain weight on this trip. Liter caught me up on the latest and

171

played the recorded phone call for me between "Fat Tony" and his nephew. "Well, fellas, it sure is a good morning. I think we have enough to arrest him with what the defendant, guard Johnson, told us and his admission on tape. Plus, we better put defendant Johnson in protective custody. Let's get him cuffed now before he gets on a plane."

"You got it. Our friends here are more than willing to help us. I'll get the extradition paperwork ready."

"Great work!"

After our meeting, I called Mrs. Rogers with the news. After giving her the update, I could hear her crying over the phone.

"Anthony, I don't know how to thank you, but my family and I will always hold you near and dear in our hearts." We got off the phone, and just then, Christine walked up.

"Anthony, you o.k.?"

"Yes, but sometimes this job can be very emotional with a little stress sprinkled on top.

"Well, I know how to fix that," as she pointed to the beautiful church. "Let's go pray."

Chapter 50

The next morning, our conference began. It was nice to see old friends and make some new ones. We had a decent agenda that included war crimes, the international sex trade of minors, and financial crimes that spread across the world. I was going to serve on a panel regarding "the drug cartels" and their influences across the southern continents. It was good timing on my part.

That morning, Liter called me and said Michael Gracciano was now in custody, and they worked it out to transport him by plane to California, where he would be arraigned in our county for the murder of Coach Rogers. Surprisingly, he waived extradition as he said, "You have nothing on me. Prove it!" Little did he know.

After the beautiful opening ceremonies, with the Italian National Anthem being sung by one of their opera stars, our meeting started. The morning was devoted to the issue of "sex trafficking" in the European countries, an issue we are very familiar with in the "states." After an excellent panel presentation, we took our first break. I went up to my room, and the message light was blinking on my phone. I picked up the receiver and hit play. It was Rachel.

"Anthony, call me back when you can; nothing urgent." Well, I was happy to hear that. I then called her.

"Rachel, everything o.k.?"

"Hello, Mr. District Attorney," she responded.

"What?"

"Anthony, the deadline to file a candidate statement was yesterday, and no one else but you filed! I think you scared them off. All kidding aside, I believe the endorsement of DA Matthews and all of law enforcement kept them away."

"Wow," I said as I sat down in a red chair in my room. "I can't believe it."

"Well, believe it, DA Garcia, but we still have to pay for a candidate's statement that goes in the voter guide, and even though your name will be the only one on the ballot, there is always the 'write-in' box. So, let's run a campaign, but we certainly don't need a professional consultant now. We should have a small fundraiser to thank our supporters and pay for a piece in the mail. Kelly agrees with me, and we think you just do your job, and we'll take care of the rest."

"Speaking of a job, I need to get back to the meeting. I love you, and high-five the kids for me."

"Yes sir, Mr. DA." Very funny.

As soon as I got off the phone, I called Liter but got his message recorder. Leave a message at the beep as I'm on a golf course. No, he wasn't. I remembered he was on a plane. I left him the following message: "Detective Dean Liter, this is District Attorney Garcia. We just put in for an 'Eagle.' Call me later."

I went back into the conference, and all my buddies saw me and said, "What's up? It looks like you just won the lottery." I went on to share the good news, and our president from Italy announced it over the loudspeaker. I received a nice standing ovation.

After the day ended, I picked up the phone and called Christine. "Anthony, that is great news. You must come over for dinner tonight, and we can celebrate."

"That sounds great."

"I'll pick you up around 6:00."

"Wonderful."

I do wish I was at home celebrating with my family, including my brother Artie and Kelly, but I guess that can wait. In fact, knowing Kelly, I can hear her now: "Tony, don't count your chicken's blah, blah, blah." However, that goes. I do love her like a sister, and she and Rachel are the original "Cagney and Lacey" and, at times, "Lucy and Ethel." HA!!

Chapter 51

Christine picked me up at 6:00 p.m. sharp. "Ciao, Anthony, I'm so glad you could join us for dinner."

"Thank you, Chris. I'm looking forward to meeting Francisco."

"You will not only meet him, but you will enjoy his food as well, as he is the cook in the family."

We approached a beautiful home surrounded by green trees and beautiful flowerbeds. The house sat on a hill with a tremendous view of Florence. The weather was perfect, so dinner was served on their back patio. Francisco was a handsome man dressed in white cotton pants and a pink button-down shirt. A "GQ" cover if there ever was one. He also had a full head of hair that I would die for.

"Pia cere di conoscerti, nice to meet you Anthony. I have heard so much about you."

I responded with the standard, "I hope good things."

"Well..." he said, laughing. He had a bottle of red wine in his hand and poured us all a glass.

"Thank you for having me."

"It's a celebration of sorts," Christine said, "As Anthony is now an elected District Attorney."

"Well, not yet, Chris, but soon."

"Congratulations, Antonio."

"Thank you."

At that moment, young Antonio walked around the corner

holding a basket of bread. "Papa, I have the 'pane.'"

"Say hello to Anthony. Remember him from America?"

"Si, buonasera signore Anthony."

"Buonasera Antonio." What a handsome young man who looked just like his mom. Big dark eyes and a mop of curly hair.

As we sat down to dinner, Chris said a prayer, and then we enjoyed a fabulous meal of sliced tomatoes, olives, and fresh cheese as an appetizer. The tomatoes were better than anything I had in America. They also sprinkled a little salt on them. The main course was a seafood pasta dish loaded with clams, shrimp, and scallops served in a bowl. The bread was warm as I dipped it into the soupy dish. "OMG, Francisco, this is delicious."

"Thank you, Anthony. I love shopping at the fish market to get the freshest catch of the day."

As we ate, I couldn't help but admire their backyard. A huge triple water fountain with beds of flowers surrounds the entire yard. It was like a Better Homes and Garden magazine picture.

We talked about the past and how Chris and I met, then the tragic day she went missing, even though she didn't. We drank more wine, and I heard about their story. It was a beautiful evening with homemade "Tiramisu" for dessert.

"Francisco, Chris, I best leave now, as I have a big day tomorrow, and then I leave for home the next day. It was nice talking about everything but work."

"Anthony, before you leave, I have something for you." At this point, little Antonio brought out a framed, covered picture. I lifted the cloth, and it was the beautiful oil painting of the little boy with the multi-colored balloons lifting him up to the sky. The note attached, "Love, Christine."

"I love you too," I said as we hugged.

PART VI
THE END

Chapter 52

The flight back home was long, but it gave me time to reflect. Christine had given me a ride back to the hotel, and she suggested that I ship the beautiful oil painting she gave me through a company that transported paintings. She told me about her inspiration for the painting.

"Anthony, the little boy is you. I have played the movie '*The Red Balloon*' for my son and for myself many times! It reminds me of the days of innocence while growing up in our little rural community. The story is about love and humanity, of course, but it also allows you to come up with an ending. What happens to that little boy? Well, he ends up fighting for victims of crime. The balloons of all different colors are the angel's victims, ascending into heaven. That's why I painted it."

"It's beautiful, Christine, and I will cherish it forever."

As she was about to leave, she said, "I'll see you soon, Anthony, as I just got an invitation to present my art at a show in Palm Springs. I know that's close to you, and I hope you can make it."

"I will be there for sure, along with Rachel and the kiddos." She kissed me on each cheek and then drove away. I do love the Italian customs.

On the rest of the flight, I thought about the future between reading the newest John Grisham novel. The plane landed at L.A.X. about twelve hours later. There to greet me was Rachel, looking absolutely beautiful with a cotton sundress on and her hair curled to her shoulders.

"Anthony, we are so glad you're home. The kids miss you, and your brother wants to come by for dinner."

"That sounds great, but let's wait until next weekend for dinner." It was Saturday, and I knew I had a big week in the office.

On the way home, I caught Rachel up on everything that happened in Italy. From work to my time with Christine and her family. Rachel talked about the plan she and Kelly put together about the DA race, or I should say "crawl," as I was the only one who filed, but that would change sooner than later. When we got home, Christine, my daughter, ran out to hug me, and Patrick was at football practice.

"Hey, sweetheart!"

"Dad, District Attorney Matthews called and asked if you were home yet. I told him you were on your way, and he asked that you call him." I looked at Rachel, and she said, "You better call him."

The phone rang once, "hello, Anthony."

"Hello, boss."

"How was Italy?"

"Very productive. I can share with you now or on Monday."

"Monday works as I have something else I want to discuss."

"Oh?"

"Yes, your future. Do you have a few minutes?" As I looked at Rachel, I said, "Of course."

"I'll be right over." DA Matthews lives in Redlands as well, and when your boss wants to talk to you in person, you say yes. My jet lag can wait. Rachel agreed.

Ten minutes later, he was at the door. Rachel answered and

invited him in. "I'm glad you're here as well, Rachel." We sat in our living area. "Would you like something to drink?"

"No, this won't take long, but thank you."

"Anthony, now that no one else has filed, I decided I would retire before my term ends. I have spoken confidentially to the members of the Board of Supervisors, and they have agreed to appoint you, District Attorney, to serve out my term prior to the formal election. The fact that no one is running against you made it easier politically for everyone." I looked at Rachel, and she looked at me. I felt like the boy and the balloons. "What do you think?"

"Boss, I would be honored to accept the position early."

"Well, good then, it's done. I'm going to have a press conference on Monday, and I want you there, so wear a good suit, not that Italian shirt you're wearing", he laughed. "You know, Anthony, it's a totally different role. You will no longer be the 'fighter pilot' trial lawyer but a manager of 500 employees, half of them attorneys. You will also have a huge role in the law and justice world along with other community commitments." He then stood and shook my hand.

I said, "I have been preparing myself for this for years, starting in high school."

"Well, congratulations, District Attorney Garcia. I'll see you on Monday. Nice to see you again, Rachel."

After he left, Rachel and I "high-fived" each other. "I must call Kelly."

"OK, and I'm going to unpack."

As I went up to my room, I realized that I would have to give up my cases. The "death row" killer had pled guilty but still wanted to talk before sentencing, but Michael Gracciano's case would have to be handed off. I then called Liter and said, "Let's meet in my office early Monday and wear a suit."

"What now 'princess'?"

"Hey, I resemble that remark. See you Monday."

Chapter 53

1975

It was the summer before my final year at Redlands High School. It was a fun summer, and I got a job as a roofer, a grueling job in the California heat. I told myself that I had to get a higher education. My brothers and I were getting ready for football season. I would be a senior, my brother Arthur a junior, and my foster brother Samuel a sophomore. My brother Artie was a lot bigger than us. He was 6'2" and a solid 200 pounds plus. He worked out with his lineman buddies. Samuel and I were both planning to play running backs, and I also wanted to continue to play defense. All summer long, we lifted weights in our summer school football class. We had weightlifting competitions against other schools and a passing league that our Q.B. destroyed. As for the weightlifting competition, I always paired up against a lineman as they paired you with your "bench press" max. I was benching 250 pounds. Not bad for a 150-pound player. The competition was not all about weights; it included the 40-yard dash, which really wasn't fair to my competition. I ran a 4.6 forty-yard dash, second fastest on the team to our standout wide receiver, Matt Brags. He could fly!

Samuel was my brother Artie's best friend in elementary school and was always at our house. He was a great athlete even back then, especially in our "John Perez" Little League. He loved the Dodgers and still does. His story is as follows: his father was an alcoholic and abusive. His mother was super nice, as was his grandmother, but it was a household full of chaos, especially after his grandmother passed away. When my dad heard about this, he and my stepmom asked if he would like to live in our home.

"Yes, sir, Mr. Garcia. I would love to live here."

My dad then met with his mother, who loved him but knew it was best. My dad said she could visit him anytime, and he kept his word, inviting her to all our holiday parties, especially the 4th of July party "Pop" loved.

That summer, Samuel and I had a mission to be in better shape than any of the other players. He was going to be on the sophomore team after a great 9th grade at Clement Junior High, where he lettered in every sport and was voted the most valuable athlete, a perfect training partner.

We started running the bleachers at the University of Redlands to get our leg strength up and our cardio going. Then we switched to the "little hill from hell," I called it. It was located next to the Greek Theater at the College and was a 200-yard hill between some beautiful trees. We would do ten intervals at full speed; it was brutal, but we were now ready for our football season to start.

The first week of practice was what we called "Triple Sessions," three practices a day. The morning session was getting the players in shape, running a "four corner drill" where we broke into groups and would run to a corner of a 200-yard field where we then stopped at each corner and did various drills, "burpees," jumping jacks, pushups, and sit-ups in the wet grass. To this day, freshly cut grass in the summer reminds me of my high school football days. Thank God I had prepared as I was leading the team around these workouts. We would then break up by positions, do drills, and end the morning session with sprints. On a side note, back in those days, we maybe had two water breaks if we were lucky. It was seen as a weakness back then. I remember after practice, we would go to the local "Taco Tia" taco place and get a huge orange soda with crushed ice; it was heavenly.

The afternoon session was more relaxed, going over plays and special team drills. However, it was tough putting on the nasty shorts and shirts, wet from the morning practice. The evening practice was the best, with full pads and physical contact. It was a time to shine. We practiced under the lights in our white practice uniforms and white helmets with the block letter "R" on the side. I loved it. The community would come out to watch us go through drills and run plays. This is where this 150-pound player literally went crazy. I loved to hit, and I believe it's how I got to start as the 150-pound defensive end and running back with a role on three special teams for the first three pre-season games.

I remember Travis Williams and I went head-to-head on several occasions. He was big, fast, and hit like a truck going full speed.

"Hey, Anthony, you're mine," he would say, smiling.

"Bring it 'T.W.,'" we called him.

Of course, at that time, I had no idea he was "juiced" up. After our last three-day practice, he put his arm around me and said, "You're pretty tough for a skinny little brown guy." We both laughed and felt good about the season ahead.

However, the best part of that year was Coach Rogers. He pushed us hard, but he really cared about us as young men. That's what he would call us, "young man." He was preparing us for life. I recall one day, he called me into his office after one of our film sessions that took place on Saturdays after our games.

"Anthony, sit down. How are you doing?"

"I'm fine, Coach." I thought I was in trouble.

"Well, good, as I just wanted to say how fun it's been to coach you."

"Thank you, Coach. I love this team."

"What are your plans for the future, Anthony?"

186

"I'm really not sure yet, but I would love to 'coach' someday."

"I'm glad to hear that. Coaching can come in many forms. Coaching sports, but more importantly, whatever you choose in life, you can be a leader and use the skills of a coach to form your team, whether it's a football team or a business or a police chief, whatever you decide to do."

And there it was, the foundation for the rest of my life. Hard work, a team concept, and leading like my favorite coach. I didn't know then how much Coach Rogers meant to me, and all my teammates were like brothers. No matter what life brings, I want it to be a team.

"Go, Terriers!"

Chapter 54

2006

Detective Liter showed up in my office at 8:30 a.m. The press conference was to start at 9:00 a.m. I had stopped at Sacred Heart Church to say a prayer and was at the office by 8:00 a.m.

"Good morning, 'Mr. DA'."

"Well, not yet, Liter, but getting closer. How was your trip back with the murderer, Michael Gracciano?"

"The fool talks a lot and thinks he's going to skate. He says he can't wait to meet you."

My old football instincts kicked in. "Bring it."

"Settle down, Tony."

The press conference was held in the media room outside DA Matthews's office. It was mostly newspaper reporters, with one camera from "ABC." As DA Matthews shared his intent to retire early, he then turned to me and said he was supporting Anthony Garcia to be the next District Attorney. Of course, the Board of Supervisors still had to appoint me, but three County Board members were there clapping as DA Matthews called me to the podium.

I walked up without a written speech and spoke from the heart:

I want to thank all of you for being here today. I am truly humbled by this opportunity. (And then it came to me. I had to stop for a second as I got choked up.)

Years ago, my coach, Coach Rogers, said you can be a leader and lead by example and as a coach. That's how I plan to run this office, with the ethics and integrity that Coach Rogers instilled in me.

Thank you.

"Anthony, is that the same coach that was murdered?"

"Yes."

"Do you have a suspect?"

"Yes, he will be arraigned tomorrow."

"Will you handle the case?"

"No, it will be assigned to one of our lead prosecutors."

"Anthony, what about the 'Death Row killings'?"

"As you know, the defendant, Tim Johnson, has pled guilty in that case."

"Does that include the inmate, Richard Cruz?"

"I can't comment on specifics at this time."

DA Matthews then stepped in and thanked everyone for being there.

Detective Liter and I walked back to my office to prepare for a full day of court the following morning. We were both still a little jet-lagged and decided nine holes of golf were in order this afternoon.

"I'll meet you around 1:00, Tony, and we can discuss our strategy for tomorrow."

As I walked up to the golf course, Liter pulled his golf cart up and said, "Get in. Folks are talking about the press conference this morning, and I thought you would need a break."

"Good call, Liter."

"Welcome to your new world."

The first hole was always my rule, "Hit until you're happy." It was good for both of us as we tended to pull our first drives. The other rule I got from Judge Sam Yo is that the first hole is a par. "We're not on the P.G.A. Tour," I reminded folks. "Oh, and a mulligan per side."

"No wonder everyone likes playing with you, Tony."

"What's the plan for tomorrow?"

"As for defendant Tim Johnson, he has pled guilty, but we were going to see what else he had to say before he is sentenced. The best would be two life terms with a possibility of parole, but I doubt that will happen as he already got a huge break that we are not seeking the death penalty.

"I still find that crazy," Liter said, "A killer killing murderers on death row, and he could have ended up there himself."

"No kidding." Just then, I hit my 3-wood as pure as ever at 200 yards out and was on the green, pin high.

"Nice shot, Mr. DA." Of course, Liter only had 140 yards to the green after his monster drive. He then stuck his wedge 2 feet from the hole. He's a hell of a golfer.

"Nice shot! I'm not sure if you're a better golfer or detective."

"How about it depends on the game, Tony, golf or justice."

"I like it."

We finished our nine holes and decided to have a cold beer in the Club House. It was around 4:00 p.m., and the news was on. There, I was getting questioned about our ongoing murder cases.

"Good answers, Mr. DA."

"How about just Tony?"

"OK, princess." We both had a laugh. It was time to go home to the family.

Rachel had to work late, and it was my turn to make dinner; both Patrick and Christine were home and hungry.

"Dad, we are tired of McDonalds. Can you whip up your special dinner?" Of course, the hot dog, bean, and cheese burritos were my specialty. Since they were toddlers, they loved them. Cut-up hot dogs fried in a pan, Rosarito beans, and shredded cheese wrapped in a flour tortilla with some red hot sauce. Even I loved them. We gobbled them down and saved a couple for "Mama"; she was also a fan. Sometimes, the simple things in life were the best.

We talked about their day, and they both told me how proud they were of me.

"It goes both ways. I'm proud of you two as well. Time for homework and to get ready for tomorrow."

They ran up to their rooms, and I had a cocktail and pondered about court for tomorrow and the future. Just then, Rachel walked in.

"I'm home and starving."

"I made you a gourmet dinner."

"Yes!! Hot dog, bean burritos." How did she know?

Chapter 55

The next morning, I did my four-mile run and grabbed my paper in the driveway to read with my coffee. Headline:

DA Matthews to Retire Early, Selects "Death Row" Prosecutor To Take His Place.

Really? Death Row prosecutor? I do have a name. I went on to discuss the case and how Anthony Garcia may have to pass off the case of Michael Gracciano, who was alleged to have killed popular Coach Greg Rogers. I got ready and then headed off to meet Liter and the team before going to court.

After meeting in my office, we all walked over to Department 1, with the exception of Detective Loftis, who went to the arraignment of Michael Gracciano. It would be a busy morning.

As we walked into court, Judge Warren was already on the bench. Attorney Tom Murphy was waiting for us, and so were a few reporters.

"Anthony, can we talk to the judge when she gets a break about our plea deal?"

"Sure, Tom, what's up?"

"My client is getting cold feet."

We sat for about a half hour; the old fans were blowing cool air on this morning, and the jury box was full of defendants facing various legal proceedings. Just then, Detective Loftis walked in.

"What happened, Raul?"

"They transferred defendant Gracciano's case to this department for all purposes. We lucked out again."

At that point, defendant Gracciano was walked in by the extra bailiffs in cuffs, wearing a red jumpsuit, meaning he was classified as "high security."

His case was called as soon as he walked in. He was being represented, at least at this time, by Deputy Public Defender, my nemesis, Vance Wright.

"Mr. Wright, how does your client plead?"

"Not guilty, your honor."

At which time, "Gracciano" shouted, "This is B.S., and I want to be released on bail."

Judge Warren tapped her watch. "Mr. Wright, please control your client."

"Your honor, can we continue this arraignment?"

"No, and bail is denied. Take the dates on the board, and we will see you at the pre-preliminary hearing."

It was at times like this I was glad I was a prosecutor.

"Mr. Murphy, I understand you and your client, along with Mr. Garcia, want a few minutes in my chambers?"

"Yes, your honor, we do."

"Follow me, bailiff. Please bring in the defendant as well." As we got up, I could hear cameras clicking.

"Counsel have a seat. We have a plea bargain for two murders and that the DA's office would not seek the death penalty."

"That's correct, your honor," I responded.

"Mr. Wright?"

"My client wants a better deal, one that would not include life without the possibility of parole, 'L.W.O.P.'"

"Why would the DA agree to that?"

"Mr. Johnson?"

"Judge, I have some more information I want to share with Mr. Garcia, but I'm terrified that I will be killed if I give any more information."

"Well, we can't guarantee your safety, but I will make sure the Sheriff keeps you in protective custody."

"Mr. Garcia?"

"Your honor, I'm not sure what else he could give us, but we are willing to listen."

"Alright then, I will put over this plea and sentencing for two weeks."

Mr. Murphy then said, "Please keep this confidential, as the 'vultures' are circling."

"I think he means the press," I said.

As we walked out, the defendant whispered to me, who killed Richard Cruz and winked.

The Judge walked out and indicated the case was continued for two weeks. As we got up to leave, the press followed us out.

"What's happening, Anthony?"

"Is he backing out of his plea agreement?" I told them I couldn't respond at this time.

We then heard in the background. "He should get a medal!" I was starting to agree with Mr. Diaz.

Two weeks passed, and with the information he gave us, we agreed to two counts of first-degree murder with the possibility of parole. The plea went down with no issues. The headline read the next morning:

Death Row Murderer Gets a Better Plea Bargain, Why?

Chapter 56

Wendy Godfried woke up as former San Quentin guard David Chavez was reading the paper in bed. "Good morning, handsome," as she liked to call him.

"Good morning. It looks like our plan worked as 'Baby Hughey' Johnson took the fall, but they are saying he couldn't be tied to the Richard Cruz case."

"That's our secret, David."

"I can't thank you enough for taking care of that murderer who killed my cousin. He was a good man and a great C.H.P. Officer. How did you do it?"

"I knew Johnson would get into the lethal drug room with a little help, and when he left, I made sure I got not just one, but two doses of the lethal drug "Potassium Chloride." I did have help crushing it up and putting it in his food. That name will remain confidential."

"That's o.k. I don't want to know."

"And you know one of the 'night walkers,' inmate McNight, victims was my cousin Holly Davis, my brother's daughter. We kept that hush, hush."

"I thought his autopsy said a heart attack?"

"It's good to have friends in high places, like the pathologist who left out the potassium chloride in his toxicology report."

"Wow, you are amazing, sweetheart."

"I don't know about that, but Governor Young called me yesterday and basically said thanks for helping me close down San Quentin, and if I win this presidential election, I will have you as the head of the Federal Prison System."

"No kidding?"

"Yep, pack your bags, David, as we are going to D.C."

Epilogue

One Year Later

Anthony and the detective team had met in the DA's conference room after the presidential election. Governor Young was now president-elect Young, and one of his new cabinet members was Wendy Godfried.

As they sat down, in walked F.B.I. Agent Hampton. It was now going to be a Federal investigation.

Michael Gracciano was found guilty of the murder of Coach Greg Rogers.

"Fat Tony" was slumped over in a plate of spaghetti after suffering a stroke.

Miguel Cruz was still slinging drugs in Miami but was still in a war with the Mexican Cartel.

Anthony was now the District Attorney. After the meeting, Anthony said, "Let's hit the golf course." Detective Dean Liter and Raul Loftis joined him. Detective Sandy Smith was promoted to Captain, and Detective Mike Jones was back at his condo in Baja, Mexico.

Just then, the phone rang. "Hang on, fellas."

"Anthony?"

"Yes." It was the president of the International Prosecutors Association, Lloyd Alexander. A member of the Crown Prosecution Service (CPS).

"Good day, Anthony. I'm calling as how would your copper friend say, 'Austin, we have a problem.'"

I laughed and said, "That would be 'Houston.'"

"What's up?"

"We have a serial killer in Europe, and we need your help."

Made in the USA
Las Vegas, NV
06 June 2024

90762078R20118